THE FIVE MATCHBOXES

After the police receive a warning of his impending murder, stockbroker Granville Collins is found shot dead in his office. The windows were closed, the door locked. The building was under police observation: no one except Collins entered, and no one left. And upon Collins' desk lay five empty matchboxes ... From this curious evidence Chief Inspector Garth of Scotland Yard is led not only to the cause of the murder, but also to a crime the Yard had labelled 'Case Uncompleted' ...

JOHN RUSSELL FEARN

THE FIVE MATCHBOXES

Complete and Unabridged

LINFORD
Leicester

First published in Great Britain

First Linford Edition
published 2008

British Library CIP Data

Fearn, John Russell, *1908 – 1960*
   The five matchboxes.—Large print ed.—
   Linford mystery library
   1. Murder—Investigation—Fiction
   2. Detective and mystery stories
   3. Large type books
   I. Title
   823.9'12 [F]

ISBN 978–1–84782–112–6

Published by
F. A. Thorpe (Publishing)
Anstey, Leicestershire

Set by Words & Graphics Ltd.
Anstey, Leicestershire
Printed and bound in Great Britain by
T. J. International Ltd., Padstow, Cornwall

This book is printed on acid-free paper

1

Beatrice Collins slowly realized that the sounds seemed to be coming from a great distance, forcing themselves upon her consciousness. Her mind gradually attuned itself from the haziness of sleep to clear perception.

'You had no right to do it! And don't let me ever catch you at it again!'

Beatrice Collins opened her brown eyes. The June morning sunshine was streaming through the imperfectly drawn window curtains. The blaze of it reflected in a blinding line along the polished edge of the dressing table and transformed the cut-glass powder bowl into a prismatic diamond.

There were sounds outside now as well as in the house, the noisy cacophony of 8 a.m. — a gate slamming, a car revving . . . They became background as a boy's voice protested in high falsetto. Back came the baritone.

'That's enough, Derek. I'm not going to argue!'

Frowning, Beatrice Collins scrambled out of bed and into her robe and slippers, hurried from the room and along the landing. The breeze from the opened window at the end of it set her thick brown hair stirring on her slender shoulders.

She found the door of her son's room wide open and hurried in — Then she stopped.

Standing by the foot of the bed, still as yet only in his dressing gown and pyjamas, was Derek Collins, tall for his twelve years, hanging his untidy dark head in something like sullen shame. He glanced up briefly at his mother's entry.

Beside the dressing table, fully arrayed in black coat and waistcoat with striped trousers, stood Granville Collins himself, an unlighted cigarette in his mouth. He was a tall, spare-shouldered man, deporting himself with something of the brooding calm of an eagle. His hands were plunged deep in his coat pockets, his austere grey eyes studying the boy. He did not even glance round as his wife came in. She found herself studying a profile of the lean face, pointed chin, the sharply hooked nose, and carefully brushed black hair with the grey streaks above the ears.

'Gran, what on earth were you shouting about?' Beatrice Collins moved forward again as she spoke and finally put her arm about the boy's shoulders.

'I lost my temper.'

'You're always losing your temper, Gran! I can't understand what's the matter with you. What was it all about? Derek! What had you been doing?'

'Nothing, mum.' Derek set his lips.

'But it must have been something, because I heard your father saying you had no right to do it, and — '

'Oh, leave the boy alone, Bee!' Granville Collins' voice was harsh with impatience as he put the unlighted cigarette back in his case. 'Confound it, why do you women have to fuss so? It's finished with.' He calmed somewhat. 'I just came in here to warn Derek that he was going to be late for school, and I found him still in bed. At his age!'

'Supposing he was?' His wife looked at him challengingly. 'It's natural to over-sleep when you're young and growing, isn't it? Was that any reason to bawl at him?'

'I didn't bawl at him!' Granville Collins snapped. 'Anyway, Derek,' — his sharp grey eyes fixed again on the boy — 'I warned you what would happen if I found you lazing again, didn't I?'

'Yes, dad,' the boy answered quietly.

'All right, then. Now get dressed and be quick about it!'

Granville Collins turned and left the room. There was an aroma of grilled bacon floating up the staircase and along the landing. He was sniffing it apprecia-tively when Beatrice caught up with him, tying the sash about her robe.

'Gran, about Derek . . .'

He stopped at the head of the stairs. 'Well — what? I'm his father — and he'll conform to what I believe is correct.'

'Oh, you and your rules and regula-tions!' she burst out hotly. 'I'm telling you straight, Gran, I'm getting about tired of it!'

4

Collins regarded his wristwatch. 'Bee, it's twenty to eight and Milly has had the breakfast waiting for quite ten minutes. I have no intention of being late even if you have. You'd better go and get dressed.'

'I'll dress later.'

Collins shrugged and led the way downstairs. Moving with sharp, precise strides he entered the breakfast room and seated himself at the table. His wife took the seat opposite him at the other end of the table and waited until the taciturn Milly had finished her maid's duties and retired.

'Bee, you look a mess!' Granville Collins said deliberately. 'You're not setting much of an example coming down like that — '

His wife's face coloured. 'Why don't you look at yourself once in a while and then try and see things as I see them? First you decided to take to sleeping in that big spare bedroom without a ghost of a proper explanation to me; then you started pitching into me for no apparent reason. You won't take me anywhere, to a theatre or anything. We've — completely lost everything we had once . . . And now you start raging at Derek. Well, that's the last straw!'

Granville Collins drank some tea with an expression of sour distaste. 'Half cold,' he complained. 'How am I supposed to improve my dyspepsia with filth like this?'

'You can't blame Milly for that. We're ten minutes late.'

'That's your fault for wasting time arguing about Derek — and he ought to be down here by now, too!'

'I — I can't go much further with this sort of life, Gran,' his wife said quietly.

Collins broke some toast noisily and regarded her. 'I told you that I took over that spare bedroom because of my indigestion, and I told you I wouldn't plant myself in a theatre or a cinema for the same reason. I need fresh air — and I mean to have it, when time allows. If because of that you start thinking it's because I'm tired of you, or some such rot,' — he smiled cynically — 'I just can't help it!'

'There are so many other things,' Beatrice said, brooding. 'Unbearable little irritations, your general irascibility. I just can't stand it!'

'I know I'm not a model man,' Collins admitted, 'and I daresay I get on your nerves sometimes as much as you get on mine. You can't sort of help that when two people live together . . . But maybe I'm going to change it.'

The air of mystery he had sought to build up for his wife was completely lost. She waited with listless expectancy.

'I think it's perhaps the house that upsets us. We've been in it ever since we were married. It's too small — produces an overwhelming crushing effect. It makes us both irritable.'

'Speak for yourself, Gran! I'm quite in love with the house, and I could be with you if you'd behave a little more sensibly and stop flying into tempers. Besides, I — ' She paused. 'You — you don't mean you have another house in mind?'

'Definitely! I'm pulling off a little business deal shortly which I'm pretty sure is going to put us on Easy Street. So far we've only been just what I call average upper middle class; if my plans work out right — and there's no reason why they shouldn't — we'll be well away.'

'Well, of course . . . ' Beatrice started to say; then at the sound of feet thundering down the stairs she made a guarded motion. 'Not a word to Derek,' she insisted. 'No reason to let him think things.'

Her husband nodded, glanced at his watch, then got up from the table. His eyes followed the boy as he entered the room at a run and then went sheepishly to his place at the table. Milly, forewarned by the din on the stairs, came in with the boy's breakfast.

Granville Collins made a half jerking motion of his dark head and his wife followed him into the hall. 'I don't mean to seem indifferent — or even bad tempered,' he said levelly, and with his grey eyes fixed on her she found it hard to disbelieve him. 'Indigestion, business worries, and — things. I married you because I loved you, Bee — and I still do.'

Beatrice Collins went to the hallstand and took down the black bowler hat from the peg. She held it before her.

'Maybe I'm — partly to blame, too,' she muttered. 'But please don't start scolding Derek again, Gran! That's one thing I can't stand.'

'I hardly think I'll need to scold him again,' Collins said grimly, taking the hat. 'And he'll be late for school if he doesn't hurry up!'

He put his bowler hat on carefully before the mirror and adjusted his tie. Then he turned, manlike, for his wife's approval.

'Just as the well-dressed stockbroker should look — except for one thing . . . ' She turned to a drawer in the hallstand and took out a white silk handkerchief, placed it carefully in the breast pocket of his coat where it reared against the black background like a snowy mountain peak.

'I don't like it,' he protested. 'I haven't worn a breast pocket handkerchief for years. I feel — conspicuous!'

'Nonsense. Just the right finishing touch.'

He studied the mirrored reflection. 'Maybe you're right. Makes a relief . . . '

The worries, the heat of words and

explosion of emotions — they had disappeared for a moment. He was Granville Collins, stockbroker, setting off for his day's business, and she was his wife seeing that his appearance reflected credit upon her management. His arm went about her slender waist for a moment as he opened the front door.

'I mean it, Bee, about something better,' he said seriously. He kissed her gently. 'Maybe we'll understand each other one of these days.'

His arm released her and she watched him walk with his swift, planned strides down the pathway. At the gate he waved momentarily, the white handkerchief gleaming strikingly against his coat — then the garden hedge hid him from her sight.

2

At eight o'clock this same morning, Chief Inspector Mortimer Garth of the Criminal Investigation Department was climbing the dingy stairs to his office in New Scotland Yard. Arriving at the Yard two hours ahead of his usual time, and with the possibility of having a hoax played upon him too, had not put him in the best of tempers.

Cheroot clamped between fleshily bulging jaws, he entered his office. Against the window, with its view of the Thames Embankment, Sergeant Whittaker stood looking out — broad-shouldered, square-faced, his ginger hair brightened with sunlight.

'Oh, good morning, sir. How are you?'

'That just plain courtesy or do you really care?' the chief inspector growled. 'Dragging a man here at this time of the morning! It'll make the day seem like ten years.'

'Yes sir.' Whittaker agreed calmly. Plainly Garth was in one of his dyspeptic moods, and that being so, anything might happen.

Short, powerful, with the body of an ox — which contrasted oddly with his emaciated face — Chief Inspector Garth slung his trilby hat carelessly on to a peg. Then, the aromatic haze of his cheroot drifting about him, he stood pondering, one hand massaging his barrel of a chest.

He had a face full of contrasts. The bulging muscles on each side of his jaw were at variance with the hollows under his high cheekbones. They made the thin, tight lips seem fuller than they really were. In one second Mortimer Garth could change his face from a relentless death mask into one of bland good humour, either mood usually being dictated by the state of his digestive tract.

'If this turns out to be a hoax, I'll publicly shoot Assistant Commissioner Sir Leonard Farley and be glad to do it!'

Garth sat down in the swivel chair at the desk and sighed. His pale-coloured eyes ranged for a moment over the correspondence and documents, then he rubbed his cliff-like forehead with the fine tracery of seams across it. Though he was only forty-eight he looked a good ten years older.

Garth tugged a small manilla envelope from the leather triangle at the corner of his blotter. He pulled the sheet of crisp, thin paper from within and reread it carefully for the sixth time. He did so in the hope that a night's rest might have brought some new mental outlook to his study of it.

The note said:

Sir Leonard Farley,
Asst. Commissioner, C.I.D.,
New Scotland Yard,
Whitehall, London.

Dear Sir,
I think you should know that Mr. Granville Collins, stockbroker, will be shot in his office in Terancy Street, London, tomorrow morning, June 11th, between 9.00 and 9.30.
Would suggest you guard the place carefully.

13

The note was unsigned and typewritten and the envelope was postmarked 'London, W.C.' for the day before at 2.45 p.m.

'We've done all we can for the moment, sir,' Sergeant Whittaker said, looking over his superior's shoulder. 'Mason is in the office building watching Collins' office, and Calthorpe is watching at the back. Calthorpe telephoned just before you got here to say that everything's in order. He's got a clear view of the back of the office building where he can see and yet can't be seen. Mason managed to get into the building when it opened at eight o'clock. Seems there is the headquarters of a motor coach company on the ground floor and they start work early on schedules and things. That gave Mason a chance to get fixed up quickly. We can trust him to have concealed himself effectively.'

'Mason, yes, but I don't trust *this*!' Garth slapped the warning note. 'In fact I wouldn't even bother with it if Sir Leonard hadn't dumped it on me!' Garth scowled. 'However, we've got to take notice of it. It may be a genuine warning of danger threatening this bloke Collins, and on the other hand it may be somebody trying to take a rise out of Scotland Yard.'

'Our hands are a bit tied, sir,' Whittaker commented. 'Unless Collins himself asks for police protection it would not be prudent for us to give it. Yet on the other hand we can't ignore it in case murder or something is attempted.'

Garth rose and put the note away in his desk drawer. 'Since the note came yesterday, it has at least given us a chance to unearth a thing or two.'

'Precious little though, at such short notice. You can't find out in five minutes if a man has any enemies or not — '

'Be damned to his enemies,' Garth interrupted, whipping his hat from the peg and planking it on his wiry brown hair. 'What does the chap himself look like? You checked up on that, didn't you?'

'Yes, sir. I did it discreetly. As the note says, he's a stockbroker and he has an office on the top floor of Amberly Building in Terancy Street. Only about two miles from here, near Throgmorton

Street. He's — er — ' Whittaker consulted his notebook. 'He's about six feet tall, dark hair, usually dresses in black coat and striped trousers. Has a wife and son. His home address is 18, Calver Crescent, Highgate. Lower end thereof.'

'All right. Not frightfully informative but it's probably all we'll need. Come on; we'll get positioned to watch the front of the building. Did you find a good spot?'

'Yes. There's a side alley opposite the building that gives a complete view of Terancy Street both ways.'

They left the office together. In three minutes they were in their official car with Whittaker at the wheel as usual. Reaching the vicinity of Throgmorton Street, he turned down a side road and drew up finally at the extreme end of it.

Through the windscreen ahead of them, and at right angles to the narrow road in which they were parked, was a clear view of Terancy Street itself. Everything was quiet.

'That's the place, sir,' Whittaker said,

nodding to a building directly facing them.

It was a three-storey structure and appeared to be an old house converted into offices. It was isolated from the less tall buildings around it. The windows were of the sash variety, one huge one to each floor. The ground floor one had a wire gauze across it with SUPERFAST COACH COMPANY displayed in gold letters.

The doorway of the building was large and arched, with a small portico in front dominated by somewhat eroded pillars. Across the top of the portico the words AMBERLY BUILDING had been chiselled. To the right of the doorway were three brass plates catching the June sunshine, though at their present distance neither Garth nor Whittaker could read them.

'That's *his* office at the top,' Whittaker added, and Garth raised his eyes to the topmost window. It was well cleaned but entirely bare as far as curtain or guardian wire-gauze were concerned.

'So far,' the Chief Inspector said, 'so

good. And I'll be hanged if I can rid my mind of the thought that this is a hoax . . . ' He slanted an eye at the dashboard clock: 8.35. 'He shouldn't be long, anyway.'

Whittaker nudged the Chief Inspector's arm and they watched a man approaching from the right-hand end of Terancy Street. It was not Granville Collins, however. The man kept straight on and vanished at the other end of the street. Other men, and once a woman, followed, apparently taking the street as a short cut to their places of business — then just as Garth was beginning to mutter irritably and the dashboard clock showed 9 a.m. a tall figure in a dark suit and striped trousers, wearing a bowler hat, appeared from the left-hand end of the street.

'I think that's *him*, sir.' Whittaker was peering hard. 'He fits the description. Six feet, black coat, striped trousers — '

'And one hell of a white handkerchief,' Garth added with a grin. 'Wonder if he feels as conspicuous as I do when I wear one . . . ? Yes, he seems to be our man all right.'

The tall figure walked with deliberate, unhurried tread along the opposite side of the street. Finally he turned in at the gateless opening of the office building, strode up the short, flagged path and so up the two steps into the hall. Then he had vanished.

Garth sat back again and pulled a cheroot from the leather case he drew from his coat pocket. 'We'll have to stay here and see what happens next. Between nine and nine-thirty the note said. Mmmm . . . we'll stop until ten. If nothing happens by then we can safely assume we've been had, but we'll pay him a call before we go to make sure.'

Though both men appeared idle, their eyes were constantly scanning the quiet, little-used street, ready for the least sign of the unusual or the presence of a doubtful looking character.

The dashboard clock presently reached nine-fifteen. So far nothing had happened. Nobody had entered the office building in the interval, though one or two people had hurried along the street, presumably on their way to business.

Garth bit hard on his cheroot and dragged down his bushy eyebrows.

'What's a word with four letters meaning brainless?' he asked, musing. 'I'm just thinking about my crossword at home. I've got to finish it this week — '

'Daft?' Whittaker suggested. 'And — ' He broke off, startled. '*What the hell's up with Mason?*'

Mason, the plain-clothes man who had been detailed to watch the inside of the building, came hurtling out of the front doorway. He raced down the short pathway, through the gateless opening and across the street. He was panting with exertion as his red, startled face appeared in the frame of the lowered window next to Garth.

'You'd better come right away, sir,' he gasped out, pointing across the street. 'Something mighty queer going on. Somebody fired a gun, I think, and I can't get any answer out of Collins' office.'

Garth leapt out of the car, jerking his head to Whittaker to follow him. 'You stay here,' he instructed Mason. 'Keep your eyes glued on that building until you hear

20

from me. Come on, Whitty.'

They hurried across the street and into the gloomy hall of the building. Then they were bounding up the uncarpeted, dusty stairs two at a time. At the top they took a sharp turn left along a landing and past the door of '*Andrew Martin, Psychologist and Astrological Consultant.*'

Breathing hard, Garth pounded up the second flight of stairs. They were lighted by diffused daylight struggling through the grimy double panes of a skylight far above, set in a slanting ceiling. So they came to another landing, bare, deserted, and cold. To the left it ended in a blank wall; to the right it was a dark, narrow vista with a wooden door, partly ajar and facing them, at the far end. Part way down the narrow landing and sideways to it was a door with a ground glass panel upon which was printed GRANVILLE COLLINS, STOCK AND SHARE BROKER.

Garth seized the doorknob and banged his fist on the wood edging the glass panel.

'Hello, there! Mr. Collins! You there?'

There was no answer. Down below on

21

the second landing it sounded as though a door were being opened creakily.

'All right, we'll break in,' Garth said briefly. 'No other way.'

He jabbed his elbow up sharply and smashed the glass panel. Reaching inside he seized the bevelled edge of the Yale lock knob and turned it. Together he and Whittaker walked into the office . . . and paused.

The first thing of which they were conscious was Collins' sprawled body under one of the windows — but automatically they also registered the broader, immediate details as well. The office was a large one, far larger than normal indeed, with two windows — one facing on to Terancy Street and the other at right angles staring over the yards and roofs of the neighbouring buildings.

A big flat-topped desk stood in the centre of the room, and beyond it in the distance a large-sized safe was raised on a brick platform. On top of the safe reposed a big tin bowl. In a far corner was a smaller desk on which stood a covered typewriter, and beside it on a folding trestle table, a Dictaphone. Then came three tall metal filing cabinets.

So it all stood, impressing itself photographically on the minds of the two men. About it all was a deadening atmosphere smelling of one thing only — dust. Then they were both looking again at the body sprawled under the window.

Taking care not to touch anything Garth prowled across the office to where the body lay. Dropping on one knee beside it he studied it carefully.

It was lying on its face, the arms thrust out over the head so that the fingertips almost reached the wall beneath the window. The feet were stretched in the general direction of the desk, the left leg bent slightly inwards.

Stooping low so that he could see the face — it was turned a little to the left — Garth contemplated it. Finally he took the pulse, shrugged, and got to his feet.

'Whether it's definitely Collins I don't know,' he said. 'But there's no doubt that he's dead. Nip down to the car and radio the Yard to send over Doc Myers, fingerprint boys, photographers, and two more PC men. I'm not touching that telephone.'

'Right, sir.'

While Sergeant Whittaker was gone Garth remained practically motionless, except once when he sniffed the air for cordite fumes and failed to detect any. He was hardly conscious of the sergeant's return until his voice broke in on his thoughts.

'What do you make of that, sir?'

Garth turned. Now he came to recall it he had seen the objects to which Whittaker was referring — in his first glance round the office, but at the time he had been too centred on the sprawled body to think further.

On the desk blotter, set down neatly in a row yet not quite touching each other, were five empty matchboxes.

3

'Good — good morning, gentlemen! Is anything — hem! — wrong?'

Both Garth and Whittaker, who had been absorbed in gazing at the five empty matchboxes, swung round.

An immensely stout man was standing in the doorway, breathing with a certain bronchial effort. There was about him a sort of geniality liberally mixed with wonder — then as he caught sight of the body for the first time he drew back a pace.

'Good Lord!' he exclaimed, putting a hand to his cushiony lips.

'Who are you, sir?' Garth asked him briefly.

'I'm Andrew Martin from the floor below. I'm an astrological consultant and psychologist.' He grew bolder, a delicate pink suffusing the fleshy folds of his face and spreading up into his quasi-bald head. 'I heard a lot of running up and down stairs and I thought I'd better see what was going on.'

'Why?' Garth asked him bluntly.

Martin spread his fat hands. 'Well, it's a quiet building as a rule.' His prominent blue eyes strayed to the figure under the window and then back to Garth. 'I — I say, he isn't dead, is he?'

'I didn't say he was, did I?' Garth's pale eyes never moved.

'No, but I sort of guessed it, just as I've guessed you are from the police. Am I right?'

'That's correct, sir.' Garth's tone softened. 'This man is dead, and I'm Chief Inspector Garth of the C.I.D. — '

'Then you'll want to ask me a lot of questions?'

'Later I shall, yes. This is neither the time nor the place.' Garth considered briefly, then: 'However, since you are here you can perhaps help me in one particular. Is this man Granville Collins?'

The psychologist waddled into the room. He seemed to be smugly pleased with himself. Coming to the body by the window he cocked his big head on one side.

'Yes, it's Mr. Collins,' he confirmed, glancing up.

'You're certain?' Garth rubbed his chest pensively.

'Quite certain. I've known him for the last six months — ever since he came here.' Martin hesitated, then turned suddenly. 'Look here, Inspector, what's going on? I'm all in the dark and that makes it hard for me to help you.'

Garth smiled and caught the ponderous psychologist by the arm. Gently he moved him towards the doorway again.

'Suppose I have a chat with you later, sir, eh? At the moment you can help me best by returning to your office and staying there. I'll be down shortly for a word with you'

'Oh, well, all right.' Andrew Martin took another sidelong look at the body, then turned and went down the narrow, dismal landing outside to the staircase.

Garth moved again to the desk, his pale eyes fixed on the five matchboxes. They were of the ordinary box variety with the label of a famous brand on the lids.

'You sent for those two extra men, Whitty?'

'Yes, sir. They'll be here any moment now.'

'Good. They can relieve Mason and Calthorpe from duty. When that happens I want Mason and Calthorpe brought up here. I don't want this building left unwatched for a single instant until it's been searched. When the two new chaps come you arrange for the relief and then make an examination of this place from cellar to roof. I'll send Mason and Calthorpe to help you the minute I've finished questioning 'em — '

Garth paused as there came the sound of feet on the stairs. It was not long before two plain-clothes men entered the office, followed by Dr. Myers, the police surgeon.

''Morning, Doc,' Garth greeted him, but beyond a brief nod the taciturn medico took no notice. Bag in hand he kneeled down beside the body.

'You two come with me,' Whittaker said to the plain-clothes men, and they followed him out on to the landing.

28

Hands plunged deep in his coat pockets, Garth began to wander round the office. At the window facing on to Terancy Street he paused, staring out on to the quiet street outside. Across the road in the side alley was the police car, a second one now drawn up behind it. Beside them Sergeant Whittaker, with the two plain-clothes men, was talking to Mason who had been left on the watch.

The chief inspector shifted his eyes to the buildings opposite. They were about eighty yards distant with their roofs at a lower level than the window out of which he was gazing. The window itself was shut and tightly latched. From the look of it, it had not been opened for years. Paint had sealed itself solidly along the edges of the frame.

Garth went over to the safe and studied its massive iron sides and door. Then he looked at the tin bowl on the top and presently at the covered typewriter — which cover he did not then disturb — and the Dictaphone.

So he came back to the desk with its normal equipment of writing pad, blotter

— and the five matchboxes, all in a row, with the trays half drawn from the lids.

'Can't do much here, Garth,' the GP said, getting up and dusting his knees vigorously. 'But I can tell you that he died from a bullet fired from a vertical position. What sort of bullet I shan't know until I dig it out.'

He motioned to where Granville Collins now lay on his back, his vest and shirt drawn to one side. Both were bloodied, though not excessively so. In the chest, directly over a line with the heart, was an oval scar from around which Myers had swabbed away the blood.

'From above, eh?' Garth repeated.

'You can see that by the shape of the wound,' Dr. Myers explained. 'If it had been straight on it would have been round. Fired from above it makes a small slit by reason of the line of traverse.' Myers was picking up his bag.

'Uh-huh,' Garth acknowledged. 'And you can't tell me anything more?'

'Not until I've made a PM, which I'll do as quickly as I can and let you have my report. Obviously,' the GP added, reflecting, 'he was shot from a fair distance. There is no powder scorching or propellant bits around the wound, as there would be from close-ranged fire . . . Tell you more, later. 'Bye for now.'

He left just as Mason and Calthorpe, sent by Sergeant Whittaker, came in.

'You first,' Garth said, looking at Mason. 'Let's have your side of it.'

'I concealed myself in the washroom at the end of the landing here, sir — that place with the wooden door — '

'I've noticed it. Go on.'

'I could get a full view of the landing from there, of course. Nothing happened — and by that I mean that nobody else came up from the moment I hid there at eight o'clock until Collins came up the stairs at nine. I noticed one thing, though: he seemed to be in a desperate hurry — '

'Hurry?' Garth repeated. 'Why should he be?'

'I don't know, sir. I heard him coming up the staircase leisurely enough. However, the moment he got to the landing he practically ran along it to the office door,

31

rattled the key in the Yale lock, jumped into his office like a two-year-old and slammed the door.'

Garth stuck a cheroot in his mouth and slapped himself for matches. 'Did you happen to hear the telephone? Maybe his haste might have been the need to answer a ringing phone.'

'I didn't hear anything like that, no.'

'Mmmm. Go on.'

'I waited to see what happened next, prepared to stay until ten o'clock and then report according to instructions. All of a sudden, though, there was a bang, a sort of sharp crack. I wasn't expecting it, of course,' Mason added in a half apology, 'so I didn't really get a chance to analyse it. But it sounded like a revolver or rifle shot. I dashed out of the washroom and banged on the office door here. Then — well, when nothing happened I came for you.'

Finding and striking a match, Garth lighted his cheroot. Then: 'And nobody else ever appeared on the corridor outside?'

'Nobody, sir. Only Collins himself came along it.'

'All right, Mason, make out your report in the usual way when you get back to the Yard and let me have it,' Garth said. 'I'll want to study it. Now go and find Sergeant Whittaker and give him a hand to search this building. He's somewhere about . . . And you, Calthorpe? What can you tell me?'

There were footsteps sounding on the stairs again just as Mason turned and went out. Calthorpe hesitated and Garth waited. It was the fingerprint men and photographers who came into the office.

''Morning, boys,' Garth acknowledged briefly, and motioned Calthorpe away from the scene of operations. They took up a position on the right of the window under which Collins was lying.

'I can't show you from here where I was standing, sir,' Calthorpe said. 'As you'll notice, the yard below has a very high wall — seven feet at least. And this building is so arranged that it has no windows at the back — only a blank face from top to bottom, with a fire escape running from yard to roof. The window — this one — and those on the lower floors corresponding to its position are at the *side* of the building.'

Garth gazed out over the huddle of converted houses and yards, the former a full storey less in height than this particular building.

'From where I was,' Calthorpe resumed, 'I could see the entire back of this place from roof to yard. The yard door was bolted, but since I was watching the only means of descent from the roof, the fire escape *and* the alley leading to the yard, I didn't think that fact signified.'

'Then you couldn't see this window?' Garth questioned.

'Not full on I couldn't, no. But I could have seen if anybody climbed into it or out of it. They'd have been instantly visible in silhouette against the sky at the edge of the building. There was nothing like that.'

'Did you *hear* anything?'

'I heard,' Calthorpe said, after meditation, 'something very much like the crack of a gun. But it seemed a long way off and I wouldn't be prepared to swear to it.'

Garth stared outside. Then: 'Why

didn't you manoeuvre into a position where you could have watched this window instead of the back of the building?'

'I had to use my own judgment, sir.' Calthorpe was defensive. 'It seemed to me, after surveying the window from a distance, that nobody could possibly get in or out of it without my seeing the silhouette. The roof is quite six feet above the window and on a slant, and the wall is sheer to the ground except for the window ledges on each floor. *But* somebody might have tried something with the fire escape, the only logical way. I couldn't watch both because of the design of the place, so I chose the fire escape as the point to watch. And until I was relieved a little while ago nobody had either climbed up or down that fire escape or appeared on it.'

Garth's eyes shifted to the dusty grey of white lead and mercury powder from the fingerprint experts' activities. The glare of the photographer's flash bulb made him blink momentarily. 'Damn me, it's impossible!' he growled suddenly. He turned and looked out of the window again upon the yards far below — quite sixty feet.

'Nobody entered or departed from this building by the way I was watching,' Calthorpe declared with conviction.

'All right, Calthorpe, I'm not doubting you,' Garth said. 'Go and find Sergeant Whittaker and tell him I want him. Take over his job of searching the building.'

'Okay, sir.'

Garth thumped his chest and shifted silently, then he glared at the fingerprint men prowling round the window. 'Going to be much longer, Smithers?' he demanded. 'I want to get that window open.'

'Won't be long,' Smithers answered impassively.

Garth sighed and strolled out into the corridor and surveyed it. Pensively, he went along to the washroom where Mason had concealed himself, and kicked the door open. Within, it was one of those gloomy, festering holes which in old-fashioned buildings come under the heading of an amenity.

One grimy window admitted faint

daylight upon dark and faded walls. There was a solitary washbowl, blackened with age, with a brass tap over it swathed in green verdigris. On a bracket above the washbowl was an empty tumbler, inverted to keep the dust out of it. In a little alcove on the opposite side of the room was an ancient type of wooden-framed water closet.

'The God-damned holes some people wash in,' Garth muttered.

He sucked hard at his cheroot so that the fumes acted as a mild disinfectant. Going to the window he rubbed away some of the grime with an old envelope from his pocket and peered outside. The view gave him an angled outlook, partly upon the back of the building and partly upon the front street. And the height was still at least sixty feet from the ground. The window was set in a solid frame, not even of the hinged variety.

At the sound of heavy footsteps the chief inspector turned suddenly to behold Sergeant Whittaker in the sepulchral daylight.

'Want me, sir?' he asked briefly.

'Yes — but I'd sooner talk in the corridor than in this rat hole.'

Whittaker followed his superior into the narrow passage outside.

'Look here, Whitty, you've got logic so badly it's almost a disease, so tell me what you think of this one: only Granville Collins came up the stairs and went into the office there. Nobody else was even seen or heard. Mason remembers a sound that he is willing to swear was a rifle or a revolver shot, and we have Collins dead in his office with a bullet wound in the heart . . . More details on that though, after the PM. He was shot from *above*. No windows were broken in the office; we know that nobody entered or left the building from the front; and Calthorpe knows nobody did from the back. He too heard something like a revolver shot but is not prepared to swear to it. This building is sixty feet up on this floor and there's only one fire escape apparently. It was in full view of Calthorpe, and is now in view of the chap watching in Calthorpe's place . . . What's the answer?'

'Offhand, sir, I'd say it couldn't be

done! There's nobody hiding in the building, at least not as far as we've discovered up to now. I've been up on the roof by the fire escape and it's as clean as a whistle.'

'Confound your clichés, man! What's the roof *like*?'

'Flat, and of concrete. There's a layer of dirt and exposure over it so that my own boots left marks that stood out a mile. And *there are no other marks* . . . ' Whittaker meditated over this. 'We'll have to make doubly sure of that fact, sir, later on. Calthorpe's going over it now with Mason to help him.'

4

Garth scowled and rubbed his chest irritably. 'I don't like these 'thin air' cases. They give me the creeps ... Anyway, until the fingerprint and photograph brigade have finished we can't poke around that office, but we can do other things. Pascal is relieving Calthorpe down in the front alley isn't he? Where the cars are parked?'

Whittaker nodded.

'All right — tell him to get off in the car to Mrs. Collins' and have him break the news to her. He'd better go with her in the car to identify the body at the mortuary. The ambulance will be here for it any time now. His wife is the best person to prove that this body *is* Collins. Radio the Yard for a fresh car to pick us up.'

'What about Martin, sir?' Whittaker questioned. 'He verified that the man's Collins, didn't he?'

'Yes, but I'm not mug enough to take the word of a stranger. Go on — hop it. You've got Collins's home address to give to Pascal. Better get Calthorpe down from the roof and have him watch the office while we go and have a word with the astrologer bloke. Mason can go on looking the place over. Leave Boardman on guard in the back entry for the time being.'

'Right, sir.'

As Whittaker went off down the narrow landing, Garth went back into Collins's office. The size of the room struck him for a moment as something of a revelation after the narrowness of the passage and dungeon-like quality of the washroom

'We've about finished here,' Smithers said, as the assistant and he packed up their equipment. 'I'll let you have the report and photographs as soon as they're ready.'

'And offhand you'd say what?' Garth picked up his hat from the desk.

'Offhand I'd say there are only two sets of prints — one whorl, ten-ridge, and one exceptional arch, nine-ridge ... We've taken prints of him, too — ' Smithers looked down at the body

Garth was left alone as the men trooped out — alone with the body of Granville Collins and five empty matchboxes on the blotter.

For several minutes he became immersed in a study of the matchboxes. He picked each one up in turn, holding it edgewise and scrutinizing it carefully. They were purely and simply *matchboxes*, but each one of them had a single small hole drilled in each end.

It was the return of Whittaker that made Garth put the boxes down again on the blotter. The sergeant came into the office with Calthorpe behind him.

'Stay here until I get back,' Garth told the PC man. 'Come on, Whitty — let's see what our obese friend has to offer.'

The chief inspector led the way down the stairs to the corridor below and rapped sharply on the glass-panelled door. The pink, round face of Andrew Martin became visible where the door had been.

'Oh, hello, Inspector. Come in.'

Garth and Whittaker followed him into an office every bit as large as Collins' above, only not quite as light. Heavy dust-ridden curtains were half drawn across the windows. What illumination there was glanced on a profoundly complex jumble of papers, books, and other paraphernalia.

Upon the walls were charts of skulls with areas marked out to denote conscious and subconscious regions. Between these charts hung pentagons, the Twelve Signs of the Zodiac, and a rather flamboyant painting of the planet Saturn.

Amidst all this oppressive over-furnishing Andrew Martin shuffled until he had two bentwood chairs clear. As Garth and Whittaker sat down in them he put himself behind the desk so that only his immensely fleshy shoulders and full-moon face were visible.

'Now, gentleman, what can I do for you?' he asked.

Garth's death mask of a face expanded suddenly into good humour. 'Just tell us in your own words all you know about the chap upstairs.'

Andrew Martin beamed as though he was enjoying being the focus of police attention. The band round Sergeant Whittaker's notebook went back with a snap as he prepared to take shorthand. Martin waited, like a conductor hovering over his orchestra in readiness for the first note.

'I've known Collins for the last six months,' he said presently. 'As long as he's been in the building. Ordinarily he kept to himself — his stock and share business, you know, but he always seemed intensely interested in my work. Once he even consulted me professionally.'

Garth raised an eyebrow. 'What about? The future?' Garth could not help sounding a trifle ironic: his reactions to Signs of the Zodiac with smatterings of phrenology and astrology thrown in had never been very cordial.

'No; it was about his mind — the mastery of fear.'

Garth alerted. 'What sort of fear?'

'Oh, fears generally. Frankly,' — Martin edged his rounded elbows forward on the desk with an air of being confidential

44

— 'he wasn't altogether clear what his trouble was. It was just a sort of generalized fear of this and that and he consulted me to see how he could better control his mind.'

Garth's eyes studied a crystal ball on its stand on the desk and a look of sour distaste crossed his face.

'People with nerves and fears usually need more iron in their blood,' said Sergeant Whittaker heavily, then he looked back at his notebook as Garth glared at him.

'This,' Martin said, with intense gentleness, 'was something of the mind. Nothing to do with the blood at all.'

'Could his fear have been engendered by the thought that somebody might want to murder him?' Garth asked.

'No, I hardly think so,' Martin shook his head. 'It was something deeper — some profound mental disturbance. I had hoped I would penetrate to the roots of his fears one day, but of course — well, he's dead, and that is that.'

'As you say, sir, that is that . . . ' The chief inspector sat back in his chair. 'Tell me, did he work alone up there or is there an office staff?'

'There is a Miss Baxter, Inspector. Very nice young lady, too.' Martin smiled and blinked at pleasurable thoughts. 'She is — or was — Mr. Collins's typist and secretary.'

'Uh-huh.' Garth reflected and looked at his watch. 'I haven't seen her yet. Since it's ten o'clock it seems to me that I should've.'

Martin agreed that it was about time and fell to scratching the folds of his chin. 'She was here yesterday — in the usual way. She came past my door at ten to nine, arriving a little ahead of Mr. Collins.'

'She has a key to the office, then?'

'I presume so.'

'Look here, Mr. Martin,' Garth said, 'you would be bound to hear Mr. Collins as he passed your door this morning . . . '

'Yes, indeed — and he passed at the usual time, about a minute to nine. Then the deliberate walk up the stairs and the hurried run along the upper landing — '

'Just a minute!' Garth's pale eyes

sharpened. 'I had one of my men posted in the corridor watching Collins, chiefly for the sake of protection, and he said what you have just said — that Collins walked sedately up the stairs and yet ran along the landing. Dammit, why should he do that?'

'I'm afraid I don't know, Inspector — but he always did. An eccentricity I presume. I suppose,' Martin mused, 'that Collins was an odd chap in many ways. I never saw a more nervous man — an uneasy sort of fellow. Sober enough in the way he did things, yet always pervaded by an air of expecting something terrible to happen. Maybe his being born under Gemini had something to do with it. June man, you know. They're the erratic type.'

'Are they though?' Garth observed heavily. 'Let's stick to essentials. What time did you get here this morning?'

'Eight o'clock. I'm always here at about that time. I write my lectures in the morning when my mind is fresh, and leave at about four in the afternoon. I've followed that procedure for years. You can ask the janitor.'

'I shall come to him later,' Garth said. 'In that case you should have heard the shot my men heard — the shot which we believe killed Collins.'

There was the sound of heavy feet tramping along the corridor outside and then going upstairs. Presumably the ambulance men. They had hardly sounded in the office above — Collins's office — before a lighter, skipping pair of feet was evident. They too raced up the stairs with all the evidences of youth, and haste.

'That's Miss Baxter,' Martin said. 'She's an hour late. Brisk, happy girl!' He sighed wistfully. 'Aries, you know, March woman.'

'If it's all the same to you, Mr. Martin,' Garth said gruffly, 'did you hear a shot?'

'Shot? Oh, yes. At least I heard *something*.'

'Can you describe it?'

'It was a sort of — of bang. But it sounded quite a distance off, and it came from above. I didn't think any more about it, of course — but I did wonder a bit when I heard that man come running down the stairs. I heard the bang, then a lot of thumping and bumping — then that man came down the stairs, tore along my landing outside and — '

'That,' Garth interrupted, 'would be Mason. The man I had on the watch.'

'Oh, would it?' Martin grinned fatuously.

Garth studied the man, trying to make up his mind whether there was here a perfectly normal man trying to be helpful and sounding suspicious in the way he did it, or whether there was something hidden behind the grins and gestures.

'You can't tell us anything more about the shot, sir?' Whittaker asked.

There was the sound of the ambulance men returning down the stairs . . .

'No,' Martin said, answering Whittaker's question. 'I can't be certain it *was* a shot I heard. Since you say so, though, it must have been. The whole business seems dreadfully queer to me.'

Garth rose in sudden decision. 'Thanks for your co-operation, anyway, Mr. Martin. Now, where can I find the janitor?'

Martin heaved and swelled to his feet

like a seal catching fish. 'He's in the basement. Not a bad sort of chap. Bit cold, though. Taurus, you know. April man.'

Garth tightened his lips and then headed for the door. Smiling faintly, Whittaker followed him and the last they saw of Andrew Martin was his pink, bobbing visage grinning cheerfully as he closed the door.

'Were you, sir, born under Saturn?' Whittaker asked archly

'Shut up, you damned fool!' Garth massaged his chest as he walked up the stairs. 'My mother always told me I was born under a gooseberry bush and it satisfies me. With a digestion like I've got I sometimes wonder why the blue thunder I was born at all . . . '

They entered the open doorway of Collins's office together. Calthorpe was still there, half seated on the desk. On a chair by the Terancy Street window sat a mid-blonde girl of perhaps twenty-two dressed in grey costume and hat. Her slim legs were crossed and a look of demure astonishment came to her face as Garth and Whittaker appeared.

Garth tossed his hat on the desk. 'You'll be Miss Baxter, I take it?'

'Yes, I — '

The girl got to her feet and took three strides from her chair; then as though she had tripped over an invisible wire her legs buckled under her and she sprawled her length on the carpet.

The thought flashed through Whittaker's mind that here was another one for the mortuary!

5

Mary Baxter was not dead, however — nor even ill. Whittaker hauled her back into the chair from which she had risen and the tumbler from the washroom, filled with cold water, did the rest. Mary Baxter began to revive from her faint by easy stages.

She kept a pair of very bewildered grey eyes fixed on Garth as he paced slowly up and down, his cheroot at an angle between his muscular jaws. She reflected that she had never seen such a merciless face — and yet how oddly it became good-humoured, almost like the face of a carnival effigy, as at length he turned and saw her watching him.

'Better?' he asked, dragging up a chair beside her and squatting on it.

'I suppose I made an awful fool of myself?' she asked quietly, colour coming back into her smooth cheeks.

Garth appraised her. She was definitely

good looking. The grey eyes were steady, the nose and lips cleanly cut. There was altogether a sincerity and youthful frankness about her.

'People usually say that when they lay themselves out,' Garth commented, grinning. 'But it's the most natural thing in the world sometimes.'

'But I never did it before,' she told him seriously. 'It must have been the utter unexpectedness of everything. I came running into the building behind the ambulance men, and then when I got in here and saw him' — she looked at the imperturbable Calthorpe now standing by the window — 'and Mr. Collins lying on the floor with blood on his shirt I . . . felt queer. But I kept steady until I stood up. Then the bottom dropped out of the earth.'

As Garth sat back in his chair, the girl's eyes shifted to Calthorpe. '*He* told me you'd be wanting to question me. You're Chief Inspector Garth, I suppose?'

'I am. And you know that your employer has been shot?'

'I know, yes.' She seemed to take a

sudden interest in studying the hem of her costume coat. 'It's awful! I can't understand it.'

Sergeant Whittaker moved silently towards the desk, sat down and tugged out his notebook.

'I understand from Mr. Martin on the floor below that you were Mr. Collins's secretary and typist?' Garth asked.

'Oh, him!' The girl flapped a white, well-manicured hand. 'He's crazy! I've no time for his stars and mental treatments, and I've told him so many a time. But he's one of those sort of people you can't insult.'

'Mr. Collins has apparently been shot dead, Miss Baxter. Have you any idea who might have wanted to kill him?'

'Not the remotest! As far as I know he had no enemies at all.'

'Most of us have enemies tucked away somewhere, young lady . . . '

'Oh, sure we have, but I mean I never saw anybody who struck me as being anxious to kill Mr. Collins. Quite the contrary, in fact.'

'The contrary?'

'Well, most of the people whom I've shown into his office to speak to him have been quite — friendly. As far as business goes, that is.'

'Uh-huh. And what kind of an employer was he? Be frank.'

'He was quite all right.' There was no hesitation in Mary Baxter's voice. 'He maintained his position and I maintained mine. I was his secretary, typist, receptionist, and so forth.'

'Did he have many callers, Miss Baxter?'

'Quite a lot — but one in particular. A Mr. Dudley Morton. He used to come on the first of every month — and has done ever since I came to work for Mr. Collins six months ago.'

'When he first started here?'

'Yes. In fact he had only just got the furniture in the office when I applied for the job. He came from a smaller office near Throgmorton Street where he said he'd been for about fifteen years.'

Garth mused. 'Fifteen years in his other office, eh? Dudley Morton? Stockbroker in a big way, as I recall . . . '

There were other things that he could recall too — unsavoury things about the conduct of Morton's business now and again, but he did not mention them.

The girl nodded an assent, then frowned slightly. 'There were some things Mr. Collins did which I could never quite understand. Sometimes he'd be as nice as pie, then at others he'd fly off the handle and rave about the smallest thing.'

'The smallest thing?'

'When we first came here it was early January. One afternoon I drew the blinds' — she nodded her head to them on their rollers at the top of the window — '*before* I switched on the lights. It was the reverse of my usual procedure: I was thinking about something else at the time. Oh, what a row there was! He fumed and raved at me for days afterwards about that, threatened me with the sack in fact. I never could understand why . . . And that's only one instance of his odd behaviour!'

Garth reflected on this, then:

'Was it part of his 'funny' temperament to run along the landing outside to and from the stairs every time?'

'That?' Mary Baxter laughed slightly. 'I don't know whether it was part of his temperament but he certainly used to do it. He always ran, and only slowed down at the stairs or the office door. Just as though — he were afraid of something.'

The good humour had gone from Garth's face and the death mask was back.

'It may have been his indigestion that made him act so — oddly,' Mary Baxter volunteered, as though she felt she had to add something. 'He suffered from it a good deal, you know. He told me that he was poisoned by something as a boy, and it permanently upset his stomach.'

'It's a general complaint, with or without poison,' Garth growled, with a thump at his chest. 'And something else, young lady — do you usually start work at ten in the morning?'

She looked abashed. 'I went to a late dance with a — a boy friend last night and overslept by an hour this morning in consequence.'

'I see. You live at home? In rooms?'

57

'At home — 45, Darlington Road, South Norwood. You see, Inspector, my parents don't entirely approve of my working for Mr. Collins — or didn't, rather. In fact they don't want me to work for anybody. But I prefer working for my living. My father does, and so does mother, even though we have private means. Anyhow, whatever chance turned up to make me perhaps lose my job they welcomed. So they let me oversleep this morning.'

'All right, so you overslept,' Garth acknowledged. 'For the moment I accept your explanation, Miss Baxter. Getting back to Mr. Collins, though: can you recall anything else about him that might interest me? His character, habits, acquaintances? He didn't, for instance, make a hobby of collecting matchboxes?'

'Matchboxes?' The girl stared at him blankly. 'Good gracious, no!' Then her eyes moved to the five empty matchboxes on the desk as Garth motioned to them. 'But — but how extraordinary! You mean they were there when you found — him?'

'I do. But never mind. Go on. So far we have his 'funny' temperament, his habit of running up and down the landing, his indigestion, and his persistent business friend on the first of the month. What else is there?'

'Well, there's one thing,' the girl said, after a long pause. 'But it's so trivial, it's hardly worth mentioning. It's about that tin bowl up there.'

The three men all looked at the bowl standing on the top of the safe. 'What about it?' Garth asked briefly.

'Mr. Collins used it for water in which to wash himself,' Mary Baxter said.

'But there's a washroom along the corridor!' Garth looked at her sharply.

'Mr. Collins wouldn't use it. He wouldn't even go and get water from it. He always made me do it — and that's the very bowl in which I got the water. Twice a day. It was part of my duties when he engaged me.'

Whittaker nearly dropped his pencil and Calthorpe in the background cleared his throat hoarsely. Mary Baxter gave a troubled little smile.

'I told you it was trivial,' she said, shrugging.

'Thanks, anyway,' Garth replied, and trivial or otherwise there was an absorbed look on his face.

'As for the rest,' the girl said, 'Mr. Collins was married and there's a son aged twelve. He lived at — '

'We know that part, thanks,' Garth interrupted, smiling genially again. 'I'm sorry I've had to question you after you fainted like that. Sure you're all right now?' He held her arm as she got to her feet.

'Yes, I'm okay again,' she assented. 'What do I do now? Go home?'

'Surely. We know where you are if we need you. I'll trouble you for the office key, though.'

She went across to the smaller desk where she had placed her handbag, took the key out of it and handed it over. Then with a final troubled look round the office she turned and went out. Sergeant Whittaker shut his notebook emphatically.

'Don't you think, sir, we might have her fingerprints?' he asked. 'If only for checking purposes?'

'We have.' Garth nodded to the empty tumbler on the desk. 'She held on to that while you gave her the water to drink. So did you for that matter but the boys'll sort 'em out. Take charge of it, will you? No reason why we should pile too much routine on the girl. She's had a nasty shock: can't blame her for dropping down cold.'

'Collins sounds to me as if he were just one jump ahead of a straitjacket,' Whittaker commented moodily.

'Maybe . . . ' Garth turned to Calthorpe. 'Hop down and dig out the janitor from the basement, Calthorpe. Bring him up here. Once he's out of the way we've got all the statements we need for the moment.'

Calthorpe went out swiftly and Whittaker idly contemplated the five matchboxes.

'Just why should any man collect matchboxes, sir? And make these holes in the ends?' He picked up a box edgewise and studied it.

'I noticed the holes,' Garth acknowledged. 'Don't ask me the why and wherefore of that now. Things are cockeyed enough already! Nobody coming or going, man shot dead, five empty matchboxes; he always washed out of a tin bowl and ran along the landing! Suffering snakes, the things I get into!'

Garth dragged out his cheroot case and had a weed in his mouth as footsteps came on the stairs. He was looking at his most forbidding and inscrutable, the cheroot smouldering gently, as the janitor was shown in.

'All right, Calthorpe,' Garth said briefly. 'Get down to the ground floor and have a word with those motor coach people. I've no time to waste on them personally. Find out what they know — if anything. Now you!' With his colourless eyes he fixed the small-built man in the overalls. He had grey hair and a hatchet face. 'You're the janitor here?'

'Sort of, sir. Caretaker really. I live on the premises.'

'What's your name?'

'Aloysius Perkins, sir — ' And in a high, thin voice the janitor added defensively, 'an' I don't like the first name any more 'n you do! I didn't 'ave no say in it, though.'

'Your name doesn't interest me in the least,' Garth told him grimly. 'It's how much you may know which counts. You've been informed what has happened here this morning?'

The caretaker nodded. 'Yes — that man you called Calthorpe told me that Mr. Collins had been shot. But I don't know nothin' about it. Gospel truth I don't!'

'Dammit, man, I didn't say you did,' Garth retorted, irritated. 'All I want from you are the answers to a few simple questions. Has anybody been in or out of this building this morning, apart from those who should normally be here?'

'That I don't know, mister.' The caretaker shrugged. 'Y'see, my quarters is in the basement an' I don't get the chance to see 'oo comes in an' out. I wouldn't know if the devil 'imself came in.'

'What time do you usually open up the building?'

'Around ten to eight. Chiefly because of Mr. Martin and the motor coach company staff. They get here early. Then I gets me brasses done outside and the steps and 'all cleaned. I — '

The caretaker stopped, his dry-lipped mouth a little agape as though he had thought of something.

'Something struck you?' Garth prompted.

'Aye — but I don't suppose it matters. You only want to know about people 'oo've come in an' out of the building.'

'I'm willing to listen to anything within reason, man!' Garth said. 'This is a murder case and I've got to know about everything that happened around this building before — and after — the crime.'

'Well, at about quarter past eight, when I was cleanin' the brass plates outside, I saw a chap standing staring at the building — an' makin' notes. I didn't think anything of it at the time,' the caretaker went on excitedly, 'no reason why I should. But 'e was there all right.'

'Can you describe him?' Garth snapped.

'Youngish. Well-dressed — sort of dapper, like. 'E 'ad a dark blue suit on, an' I think a grey soft 'at.'

'And he didn't come into the building or ask any questions?'

'No; nothin' like that. He finished

whatever it were he were writin' and then went off down the street.'

Garth took his cheroot from his mouth. 'Anything else? You can't give me any particulars about Mr. Collins?'

'I 'ardly ever saw 'im — an' 'e certainly never came down to the basement. 'E always sent that young lady clerk of 'is if anythin' needed fixin' in his office.'

'All right, that's all,' Garth said. 'You can get back to your work.'

After the caretaker shambled out, Garth turned to where Whittaker was putting his notebook away.

'Hop down and tell Boardman who's watching the back of the building to try and trace this chap in the blue suit and soft hat, Whitty. Tell him to get Mason down from the roof to help him and to send out a general call to the Yard. I've got to get hold of him: he may be useful.'

Whittaker went stolidly from the room.

'Why the devil couldn't somebody have come into the building and given me a chance to knock some sense into this cockeyed setup?' Garth asked himself bitterly.

He looked at the bunch of keys attached to the silver chain lying on the desk, which with the wallet beside it had been taken from the dead man. He picked the wallet up and then put it down again as there were footsteps on the stairs and along the landing. Calthorpe came in.

'Nothing to be squeezed out of the coach company, sir,' he announced, shrugging. 'They haven't the least idea what has been going on. There are three of 'em down there — two women clerks and a man manager. They seem to be telling the truth, and — '

'All right, never mind.' Garth made a bothered movement. 'Leave it for the moment and tell me something else. You've examined the roof? No sign of anything?'

'Nothing at all. It's a sort of flat well and made of concrete. Thick with dirt, but there are no marks of any sort either on the roof or the surrounding parapet. I've been through the building too, and drawn a complete blank.'

'All right,' Garth said sourly. 'I'll double-check it myself later on to make sure. Must be something, somewhere. A man can't be shot without somebody doing it ... Anyway, I've detailed Boardman to try and trace a man who was seen hanging about here at a quarter past eight this morning. Better go and give him a hand. Boardman can't have got far: Whittaker's only just gone to tell him.'

Calthorpe nodded and left. Garth settled down at the desk and sat with palms flat on the blotter, surveying the five matchboxes with fixed intentness. Then he picked up the wallet again. The contents he tipped out and examined them individually.

There were four currency notes, a snapshot of a straight-featured, dark-haired woman and a boy of about seven; several clipped cuttings on stocks and shares from the *Financial Times*, four sheets of blank paper presumably for notes; and yet another news-cutting dated five years previously and giving an account of one Frederick Catlow, who, charged with blackmail, had been acquitted. Briefly, the news-cutting summed up the case for the defence and gave the name of the counsel who had secured the exoneration.

Brooding over this last item particularly, Garth gathered the contents of the wallet together again and returned them to their places.

Again he looked at the five matchboxes, and then picked up the bunch of keys. By trial and error he found the one for the desk drawers and opened them. Only stationary came to light, including blank document forms for the stockbroking business, together with other standard office equipment.

Garth picked up one of the blank sheets and held it to the light for the watermark. It did not tally, in so far as he could remember, with the sheet of paper on which the warning note to Assistant Commissioner Farley had been written.

Getting up, he went over to the typewriter and flung back the cover. With one finger he typed out, practically word for word, the message of warning and was still studying it when Whittaker returned.

'That's fixed up, sir,' he announced.

'Maybe we'll get some lead on this lot if we can trace that chap.'

'Maybe,' Garth acknowledged, looking up. 'I've been looking at this typewriter. It certainly didn't type the warning note, and I don't think it was written on this sort of paper. I'll check it, anyway.' He thrust the typed sheet in his pocket and gave a snort.

'Take a look through that wallet, Whitty, and tell me what you think of the contents. I'll see what there is in the safe.'

He took the bunch of keys from the desk and again by trial and error found the appropriate one for the safe, swinging the heavy door wide. Going down on one knee he began to draw out the contents, setting them down in orderly piles in front of him . . .

At the desk Whittaker took each item from the wallet and studied it circumspectly.

'Nothing much here, sir,' he commented at length. 'I'd say the photograph is an old one of his wife and son — the boy is obviously not twelve years old here. As for the press cutting about blackmail: I don't get it. Unless the man Frederick Catlow, accused of the blackmail, was a friend of Collins . . . '

Garth merely grunted. To Whittaker's surprise, now he came to notice, his superior was squatting on the floor, leafing through the pages of a grimy book without covers.

Silently he moved and gazed interestedly over Garth's shoulder.

6

Garth aimed a pale eye up at him and grinned. 'Not exactly what you'd expect to find locked away in a safe, eh? A book ten years old, according to the publisher's date, and no title since the covers have been torn off. And of all the concentrated, unadulterated bunk — ! Look at it!' He waved it in the air like a tattered flag. ''How to Master Your Fears!' and 'The Art of Will Power' — ' He paused, frowning, and looked at the book again. ''How to Master Your Fears' — The pages of that chapter are so dirty you could sow spuds in 'em. Here, take a look.'

Whittaker grasped the book and went over to the desk with it. He browsed through the pages with that earnestness indigenous to him while Garth sifted through the rest of the documents. Practically all of them were stock and share business and involved so many names it would have taken months to docket them all. So he sidestepped them and sharpened his interest again as a bank pay-in book came to light. Pensively he studied its pages then began a hurried search through the pile of books and papers until he had dug out as many as twelve pay-in books. The whole pile he carried to the desk and began sorting them out in numerical heaps.

Pointing a red finger at the book on will power, Whittaker said: 'More I see of *this*, the more I become convinced that Granville Collins was plain barmy, sir!'

Garth did not answer him. He was searching through the pay-in counterfoils, and whatever investigation it was he had undertaken for himself it kept him occupied for twenty minutes. At the end of that time he was drawing cheerfully at the stub of his cheroot.

'That's better!' he declared, sitting back. 'At last we have something that makes a bit of sense! For the past fifteen years Collins has banked with the Consolidated,' — Garth waved a hand to the pay-in books — 'which of itself is not important, of course. What *is* important is that on the third of each month he paid the sum of one thousand pounds into the bank in high denomination notes.'

Whittaker gave a start. 'Why of course! That chap who has been here on the first of the month — ' He tugged out his notebook and scanned back through the pages. 'Dudley Morton!'

'Right,' Garth acknowledged. 'We don't know yet if Morton has paid a thousand pounds to Collins every month for fifteen years, but it's a logical inference. That will bear a good deal of examination, particularly since the man's Dudley Morton. From what I hear he doesn't play the stockbroking game as squarely as he might . . . '

'Nice money — if you can get it,' Whittaker murmured.

'According to the cheque book counter-foils, Collins lost most of his money as fast as he got it in Stock Exchange speculations,' Garth said. 'And the passbook shows he was sinking pretty low on the rocks.' He scowled at the scattered deeds on the floor.

Garth collected the pay-in books in a bundle and with the rest of the stuff returned them to the safe and closed the heavy door. For some time he wandered round, trying to find where the biggest key on the ring fitted — without result. It was a big key too, perhaps three and a quarter inches long and of the solid variety.

'No go,' he muttered, dropping the bunch back on the desk with a metallic rattle. 'Belongs to something at his home maybe. We'll have to find out . . . ' Then as he looked at Whittaker he asked dryly: 'Learned to hypnotize yourself yet, Whitty?'

'I don't understand it!' Sergeant Whittaker complained, getting up. 'Why should a man keep a ten-year old book like this in his safe, of all places? Far as I can make out it's written by some obscure professor of psychology who guarantees that you can become a mental marvel in a fortnight if you'll only follow his instructions.'

Garth stubbed his cheroot in the ashtray. 'There has to be a reason for keeping it in the safe. I'll not even hazard a guess at this juncture, but I noticed it was most soiled at the chapter on 'How to Master Your Fears' . . . ' He took it from Whittaker's hand and stuffed it in his coat pocket. 'Well, so far, so bad. Now what else have we?'

'You don't suppose,' Whittaker said absently, 'that our pink-faced friend Andrew Martin has any connection with this book, do you? Name of the writer in the title page is Abner Hilroy — but that could be assumed.'

'I don't suppose anything,' Garth answered stolidly. Rubbing his chest fiercely he went over to the window under which Collins had been lying and studied it carefully, shading his eyes against the glare of June daylight. The window was not latched, but it might have been for the effort it demanded to try and raise it.

Shoving and straining, his fingers under the looped bands of brass at the bottom of the frame, he heaved it up halfway and then stuck his head through the opening and peered outside. Whittaker's square, enquiring face appeared beside him and in silence they contemplated the view.

Above them — quite six feet above as Calthorpe had said — was the stone edge of the roof parapet. To either side for a distance of about thirteen feet on the right and eight feet on the left was blank wall without even a single drainpipe. And below, a sheer drop to the dirty little yard with its unimposing array of three well-filled dustbins.

'Did you say something about 'impossible'?' Garth asked, wheezing as he withdrew his head into the office.

Whittaker took hold of the window sash and it came down with an ease that was startling compared to the struggle it had been to raise it. Garth seemed to consider this fact for a moment, fine lines of thought on his forehead . . . then the window slid gently into place.

'He certainly wasn't shot from here,' Whittaker said seriously, turning.

There was somehow a feeling of tension, a conviction that something had happened here which could not happen under any normal conditions.

'There's that, sir,' Whittaker pointed to

a ventilator about four inches square, open so that they could see the daylight beyond it. 'If that should coincide with a position on the fire escape it's a possibility as a firing point.'

'And a thin one,' Garth said gruffly. 'We'll check on it anyway, when we go up to the roof.'

Together they continued walking along beside the walls, pausing again at the window facing on to Terancy Street. Outside, a squad car had just drawn up in response to Whittaker's request of a little while earlier. An examination of the window only confirmed Garth's original opinion that it had not been opened for years and that the paint had sealed it in. In fact, whichever way they considered the problem it had an unpleasant habit of making itself all the more obscure. The office was not overlooked in any way. It was a full storey higher than the neighbouring buildings, and the nearest of these was eighty yards away across Terancy Street.

Opposite the other window, where Collins had been lying, the nearest buildings were a good two hundred yards distant because of the intervening back areas. And all of them were low down. This particular structure stood out like a lighthouse amongst its neighbours, only matched by the distant buildings rearing near Throgmorton Street.

'And not even a blasted chimney,' Whittaker said at last. 'Just that . . . ' And he nodded to the extinguished electric radiator in the corner.

Garth peered round the office, in his grimmest mood. When he became bewildered he automatically became inscrutable and bad-tempered simultaneously. One word might explode him into real abuse.

He stared up at the ceiling. Except for the single flex where the electric light depended it was unbroken. He looked at the floor. It was boarded, polished, and solid. No loose planks or means of getting to the electric lamps that hung in the office below — Andrew Martin's abode . . . Even under the mats that Garth whirled aside there was no break in the floor.

'Plaster ceiling with presumably stone

78

above it,' he said at length. 'Floor hasn't been disturbed or prised up for donkey's years. Not a window broken or a bullet scar anywhere — suffering snakes, am I enjoying myself!'

It was one of those moments when it was not wise to comment.

'This place,' Garth said at last, half sitting on the desk and looking pained, 'wasn't rented cheaply. In fact . . . it's out of all proportion. Collins had only a moderately good business. The kind of business that could be nicely packed into a small back office instead of into a miniature ballroom like this.'

'Is there any special significance about that fact, sir? I can think of lots of reasons why he took this office — *a*: it might have been the only one vacant near to Throgmorton Street, where most of the finance is handled anyway; *b*: the rent might be far lower than one imagines because of the age of the buildings; and *c*: it may — '

'All right, all right!' Garth waved an impatient hand at him. 'I'm only airing opinions . . . Tell you what you do. Fetch one of the boys up from the squad car outside and have him stay in this office until relieved. Take this tumbler with you and put it in the car. Don't smudge it either; it may prove useful. When you get back we'll have another word with Martin and then go up on the roof.'

As Whittaker went with the tumbler held carefully, Garth turned to the desk and picked up the five matchboxes by the edges, dropped each one into a cellophane envelope and then stuffed them in his pocket. Next he collected the keys and the wallet, then settled his hat firmly on his head.

He was still prowling round the office, meditating, when Whittaker returned with the uniformed constable beside him.

'Stay here until you're relieved,' Garth instructed, and jerked his head to Whittaker. Together they went down to the psychologist's office and Martin admitted them with the same pink, bouncing, fleshy cordiality as before.

Garth shook his head at the offer of chairs. 'Thanks all the same, sir, but we're not stopping this time. I just wanted to ask a favour of you.'

The round blue eyes shone lustrously. 'I'm only too glad to help the police. What can I do?'

'Let me type a short note on your typewriter over there.' Garth nodded to it.

For a moment there was silence as the psychologist hesitated noticeably, though it was unclear whether it was suspicion or surprise that was causing it.

'Of course,' he said finally, nodding his round head. 'Go ahead.'

'Thanks.' Garth went over to the machine. He picked up the top sheet of a pile of blank paper beside the typewriter and plugged out a sentence recalled from a typewriting manual —

A quick movement of the enemy would jeopardize six gunboats.

Then he stuffed the paper in his pocket.

'I suppose,' Martin said, glowing with smiles again, 'that this is what you would call 'irregular', Inspector?'

'You've been so co-operative with us so far, I thought you wouldn't mind,' Garth said rather gruffly. 'If you hadn't agreed to my just using your machine I might have had to get the authority to force you to do so later — and I don't like throwing my weight about if I can help it.'

'The cautious, retiring type, eh?' Martin was nodding sagely. 'Tell me, inspector, were you born in October under Scorpio?'

Garth paused momentarily in the doorway and caught the repressed smile of Sergeant Whittaker

'No. I was born in November — under protest! Thanks once again, Mr. Martin. I've no doubt we'll meet again.'

Garth made an urgent nudging motion with his elbow and headed down the landing to the second flight of stairs and so to the ground floor.

'Incidentally, November man . . . ' Sergeant Whittaker paused heavily and met a glare.

'Sorry, sir — but that psychologist-cum-star-gazer tickles me pink. However, I was going to say — what about this coach firm, and their typewriters? You are, I take it, looking for the machine which typed the warning?'

'I'm not looking for it in a coach company's office because from all I've heard I don't see how they could possibly have had anything to do with this business. Or Martin either — but since he's only one floor below I'm more wary as far as he is concerned. If we need to test the coach company's machines we'll do it later. Now let's get on the roof via the fire escape.'

They went down the four steps and round the building to the back, across the dirty, untidy yard — after Whittaker had leaned over and unlocked the gate — to the fire escape. Wheezing and cursing his digestive tract Garth began to climb, looking about him as he went. Laboriously Whittaker came up behind him. Then about six feet from the top they paused as Garth pointed.

'There's the ventilator, Whitty. And if any man could see through that to aim at his victim, much less fire a revolver and kill him, I'm the angel Gabriel. That's right out! Just as we'll be if we can't knock some conceivable sense into this whole crackpot business.'

He climbed up the remaining iron steps and finally threw a leg over the stone parapet and stood contemplating the roof.

It came as no real shock to find that the flat concrete roof with its single dirty skylight — which illumined the stairs leading up to Collins's office — was solid concrete with a flat stone parapet. Calthorpe and Whittaker had both said that it was, but now the fact was substantiated there was again that sense of frustration, that leering conviction that something had happened which couldn't happen.

Whittaker pointed to the filth of exposure with which the roof was covered. 'Those smears are from my boots — or else the boys'. It was undisturbed at first.'

Garth went over to the parapet directly above Collins's window and peered below. The window was there, six feet down. 'Obviously nobody did any shooting from here,' he said sourly. 'And if they had done the window would have been broken by the bullet ... And we saw

Collins walk cheerfully into the building!'

Whittaker, usually renowned for Having his feet on the earth, actually gave a tiny shudder as a breeze played across his face: it reminded him of a playful spirit frisking past. Collins had been alive when he had entered the building, and dead when found — and nobody had ever been near him in the interval. And the only clue — if clue it could be called — was five matchboxes with holes in the ends of the trays. The sheer impossibility of the crime was giving him the willies.

He saw that Garth was now considering the dirty skylight. He went over and joined him. The dirt was untouched and the glass held in place by rusted nails that had been there for time immemorial.

'There's the inside of the building, sir,' Whittaker said, not very hopefully. 'We might take another look round.'

'We're not going to, but I'll detail Jessop and Finnigan to tear the place inside out,' Garth answered slowly, clenching his fist. 'I'll tell them the minute we get back to the Yard . . . I'll have the place taken apart brick by brick if need be ... Now let's get moving. There may be a ghost sitting in my swivel chair waiting for me ... '

7

There was no ghost at the Yard waiting for Garth's return. On the way in to his office he gave Jessop and Finnigan their orders and had hardly been in his office three minutes before Pascal arrived. Anything less phantomic than the six-foot-five Pascal could hardly be imagined. Whittaker left the office with matchboxes, wallet, and keys in one hand and his fingers straddling the tumbler in the other.

'And tell 'em at Dabs that I want to know everything about 'em as quickly as possible,' Garth called after him. 'Tell 'em to put their findings in with the rest of the reports.'

'Right, sir,' Whittaker called back from the passage, and the door closed.

Garth sat back in his swivel chair and fished in his cheroot case. 'Well, Pascal, how did you get on?'

'Quite all right, sir. I drove Mrs. Collins

to the mortuary as you instructed and she positively identified the body as that of her husband. I didn't take a personal statement, though: I thought you'd want to do that.'

'You thought right.' Garth found a match and scratched it on the box viciously. 'How'd she react?'

'She didn't seem quite as stunned as I'd expected. I broke it to her gently and prepared for a swoon. But beyond looking a bit strained and perhaps going a bit paler — hard to tell with make-up on her face — she just said quite calmly that she'd come with me. And she did.'

'You had her sign a statement to the effect that the body is that of her husband, I suppose?'

Pascal felt in his pocket and laid a folded sheet on the desk. 'All there, sir. Then I took her home again and told her to await developments.'

'Okay. That's all for now.'

Pascal went out and Garth pressed a switch on his interphone. In another moment he was through to 'Crow', the Criminal Records Office.

'Take a look through your index and let me know if you have anything on a man named Dudley Morton,' he said briefly. 'Call me back.'

He switched off and sat with his brows down; then he shifted position only to find a hard wedge at his side. Feeling in his pocket he pulled out the book on Will Power and tossed it on the blotter. Setting his teeth hard on the cheroot he stared at the ancient edition fixedly.

The office door opened and Sergeant Whittaker re-entered. He went across to his own desk in the corner, pulled out his notebook and studied it.

'Shall I get these statements typed out, sir?' he enquired.

Garth glanced at his watch. 'No, we — '

He broke off as the interphone buzzed. A voice spoke: 'Nothing on anybody named Dudley Morton, sir.'

'Right.' Garth switched off again and got to his feet, put Collins's key bunch in his pocket and locked the wallet in a drawer of his desk. 'You can finish those statements later, Whitty. We're going to get some lunch and then carry on to Mrs. Collins's to see if she can shed any light.'

Whittaker followed his dyspeptic chief out of the office. They had lunch at the *Welcome Café* and then drove out to Collins's home, arriving finally at 18, Calver Terrace, an outcropping of suburbia, a street of gauntly severe houses of definitely dated architecture. The maid Milly answered the ring at the bell and, evidently anticipating the event, she immediately showed Garth and Whittaker into the drawing room.

They seated themselves with hats on their laps, waiting, surveying the definite excess of furniture. It was a curious room, really — overweighted in every sense as though ancient and modern were locked in silent combat and neither could force the issue.

Then Mrs. Collins came in, dressed in a frock of some dark red material with a biscuit-coloured collar at the neck. Her thick dark hair was drawn back from her forehead and piled high in waves and curls on the crown of her head. The effect was to accentuate the small preciseness of her features.

'Ah, good afternoon, Mrs. Collins.' Garth got to his feet with Whittaker. He was smiling gravely, all the set hardness of the death mask ironed out for the occasion. 'I'm sorry to have to bother you at a time like this, I'm afraid. This is Sergeant Whittaker.'

Mrs. Collins shook hands with both of them and smiled faintly.

'Please sit down, gentlemen.' She settled herself in an armchair so that she faced them both. 'I suppose you want details about my husband? Fortunately I've had a little opportunity in which to compose myself, since identifying him this morning.'

She paused for a moment, her only sign of emotion the nervous plucking of her fingers at the relief design on her dress cuffs.

'I can't go into the exact circumstances of your husband's death, Mrs. Collins, since that is entirely police procedure,' Garth said. 'But I think you are the only one to help us solve some of the queer sidelights on this case . . . Was he, would you say, a man of sober outlook?'

The woman made the kind of gesture that implied she was throwing everything overboard. With sudden intensity she began to underline her words with swift movements of her hands.

'I've obviously nothing to gain by keeping back the truth about my husband,' she said, her eyes straying to Whittaker as he took out his notebook. 'He was a strange man, and of late he seemed to have become eyen stranger. His behaviour made him a difficult man to live with, though in general he was I suppose a satisfactory husband and father . . .

'When I first married my husband sixteen years ago he was considerate, kindly, had good prospects with stocks and shares. Then gradually — so gradually that I cannot recall when it all began — he seemed to change. He had always been the sensitive type, but he let it go beyond mere temperamental outbursts into utterly unaccountable behaviour. He developed, as it were, a deep inner fear, and despite all my efforts he would never explain to me . . . '

Garth and Whittaker exchanged looks; both thinking of a book on will power which had been locked away in the safe of Collins's office.

'It led to a growing estrangement between us,' Beatrice Collins went on. 'Some years ago, for instance, when this strange metamorphosis of temperament first became noticeable to me, he suddenly decided that he would have a bedroom to himself and promptly took the spare room, which we had never used up to then because of its very barrenness. For many years he slept there, right up to last night. I grew used to it, of course, because I had to — but I didn't like it.'

'He gave no explanation?' Garth asked, puzzling.

'Oh, he gave one, yes — of sorts. He said that his indigestion made it necessary for him to sleep in another room alone so that he could get plenty of air.'

'That, madam, I cannot credit!' Garth declared. 'I suffer from that complaint myself quite a lot, but I'm willing to wager that I'd land in a divorce court or something if I dared tell my wife I was taking over a separate bedroom on that account . . . Was there not some *other* reason?'

'None that he ever mentioned . . . ' Beatrice Collins said. 'Even if that explanation was right, certain other things can't be put down to dyspepsia. For instance, before this bedroom business came up we often used to go to a theatre or cinema together and left Milly to look after the boy. Then it suddenly stopped. Gran refused to do it any more. He seemed to be possessed with a sudden mania to be outdoors, and usually by himself. He even failed to renew his bus contract, refused to have a private car — though when we were married he did have a little open two-seater — and instead walked everywhere, even to his office. In fact his walk to the office was something of a ritual with him.'

As he listened to her story, Garth felt very much like a mountain climber trying to get a grip on an icy acclivity. After a moment or two she went on talking in the same listless tone.

'Last Christmas I gave him an expensive small lacquered box, in which to keep studs and links and so forth, which he was always mislaying. I thought he'd love it, but he just snatched it from me when I opened the lid to show him the inside and flung it across the room. It smashed, and he burst into a towering rage that made all my Christmas — and Derek's too — a complete misery.'

There was a hard inflexion in Mrs. Collins's voice now at the acrid memory. Garth raised his eyes to look at her and for a moment Whittaker read an intense interest in the chief inspector's emaciated face.

'Those,' Beatrice Collins said, shrugging, 'are just instances. I can't say I was stunned by the realizalion that Gran was dead. Only this morning, though I tried to put a good face on things, I was racking my brains to decide how I might make a break — ' She was suddenly urgent again. 'You see, I'm still young and, I suppose, ambitious up to a point. Though my husband had promised that he would improve our position shortly I — '

'He — what?' Garth interposed gently.

'He said that he would make things better. He had plans for a deal or something — and it involved a new house and better social advancement all round. I told him that I didn't want a new house, only for him to behave like a normal man.'

'And that was this morning?' Garth asked.

'Yes. Though I was ready for the letdown which I felt sure would come. He'd always made those sort of promises when I had shown signs of getting restive. It was just another effort to mollify me. If, of course, it had have come off I'd have been the first to welcome it. I want to climb; I aspire to something much higher than this old-fashioned house.'

'Why, if you and your husband were so much at variance, didn't you seek a separation?' Garth asked.

'Because of the boy, Mr. Garth. He's young, and impressionable. That is why I put up with so much — but thank heaven

I shall not have to any more.'

'You have said that this morning you were thinking of making a break,' Garth remarked. 'Was there any particular reason for it?'

'Definitely!' Her hands bunched into small fists. 'I was awakened this morning by my husband's voice raging at Derek. I thought something dreadful was going to happen so I dashed in to see what was wrong. All it turned out to be was that Derek was still asleep when he should have been dressing for school.'

Mrs. Collins's voice had been become quieter as if she was feeling her way backwards to something half forgotten.

'There was something odd — even grim — about the way my husband warned Derek against oversleeping. He told Derek that he knew what he'd get if he lazed again, but somehow — ' Beatrice Collins pressed finger and thumb to her eyes and shook her dark head. 'It seemed to me that there was something *else* against which he was warning Derek. I mean, the boy has overslept before and his father had been aware of it and merely treated the matter, rightly, as a trifle. I felt that this morning's affair was a — a cover-up!'

'Hmmm — and concern for your son made you flare up again against your husband. Well, that's logical. In what mood did he leave here?'

She smiled wistfully. 'Oh, we patched it up again. At least I pretended to, for the sake of peace and his promises for the future. I played the interested wife role, and felt quite a hollow sham while I did it. I gave him his hat, put him a nice white silk handkerchief in his breast pocket to convince him that I really was interested in his appearance. He wasn't best pleased for he never wore one as a rule — and then off he went. And Derek departed for school shortly afterwards. I spent this morning trying to think of some way out of the mess, then that man came from Scotland Yard and told me . . . ' her voice lowered, ' . . . told me what had happened.'

'And you were here all that time?' Garth asked.

Her dark eyes flashed. 'Yes, I most

certainly was! The maid can prove it.'

'Sorry, madam,' Garth said dryly. 'Merely a routine question. But, this business about your son has me a bit worried. If there was some other reason for your husband's outburst I'd like to know what it was. When could I see the boy?'

Beatrice Collins glanced at the clock. 'He won't be home from school for another hour and a half yet — and incidentally, gentlemen, I haven't told him yet what has happened. I'd planned to tell him tonight, in my own way.'

Garth nodded. 'I appreciate that, and I don't wish to upset things in any way. What I would suggest is that you explain to the boy what has happened when he comes home and then bring him along to Scotland Yard this evening — to my office, say about seven o'clock. I'll be working late. If there is anything else behind the 'oversleeping' theory he'll tell it quick enough with the walls of Scotland Yard about him. Or I don't know boys!'

'I'll do that,' the woman agreed. 'I'm as anxious as you are to have everything straightened out.'

'Now . . . ' Garth hunched forward, 'there are other things. When your husband was found in his office there were five empty matchboxes with holes in the trays spread out on his desk. Have you any idea what that could mean?'

'Five empty matchboxes?' she repeated in amazement. 'I haven't the slightest idea what they could mean. My husband used matches, of course, in preference to a lighter . . . I don't think he had any matches with him this morning. I remember now that when he was scolding Derek he was standing by the dressing table with an unlighted cigarette in his mouth, and finally he put it back in his case. I just don't understand it.'

'What brand of matches did he use?' Garth asked, and she gave the same name as the brand on the five matchboxes. 'And did he, as I'm afraid I do at home, scatter his empty matchboxes about the house?'

Beatrice Collins shrugged. 'I suppose that he would. Milly does the tidying, of course. Does it mean anything?'

'It may, it may not.' Garth spread his

hands. 'Now there's something else . . . '
He felt in his pocket and brought out the
bunch of keys. 'These are your husband's,
of course.'

She nodded as she looked at them.

'I've found that each of the keys fits
something in his office — except this
hefty one. Have you any idea to what it
belongs?'

'Sorry, no. I'm sure it isn't anything in
the house here; I have keys for everything.
Must be something private. My husband
was always anxious about his keys;
another of his little foibles. He used to
clip that chain to his bed mattress at
night. Once he lost the bunch and he
nearly went frantic until they were
returned.'

'Hmmm, I see.' Garth frowned as he
returned the key to his pocket. 'Now a
different question: Did your husband ever
run about parts of the house, and walk
sedately in other parts?'

'Why, really, Mr. Garth — !' An incredulous smile crossed the woman's face.

'He did so at his work, I assure you.
Always ran along the landing and yet

walked calmly up or down the stairs. He always washed from a tin bowl in his office — his typist getting the water — but he never went in the washroom. A poky little hole, incidentally.'

'All this sounds absurd to me,' Beatrice Collins declared, with a touch of anger. 'My husband was peculiar in his habits, yes, but he wasn't crazy, and never behaved like that at home here.'

'Have you any reason to suppose, Mrs. Collins, that your husband was afraid of somebody? Or of enemies generally?'

The answer was unexpected. 'Yes; but I don't know of whom. He always kept a revolver beside him at night. He said it was for protection against burglary but I often thought that it might be for some other reason. It used to be on the table at our bedside, then when he went into a room of his own he transferred it to a table there within reach of his pillow.'

'You know, of course, that it has been illegal for many years for him to have had that gun? I can only presume this was unlicensed?'

'Yes; I suppose so. I don't know much

about it, Inspector. He had it quite sixteen years and started using it shortly after we were married. I think it is a thirty-eight, or something. You'd perhaps like to see it?'

Garth nodded grimly. 'I'll do more than that: I'll call it in as unlicensed property. Naturally there will be no reflection on you.'

The woman looked at him pensively for a moment, then she got to her feet and left the room. Whittaker laid his notebook aside and flexed his wrist.

'Collins,' he said in a low voice, 'seems to have been peculiar, sir! You don't suppose he was a sufferer from Schizophrenia? Split personality?'

'No, I don't,' Garth answered calmly. 'I prefer to regard that complaint as a very overworked gag invented by Robert Louis Stevenson.'

Presently Mrs. Collins returned with the revolver. Garth took it from her and broke it open. It was a very old Smith and Wesson — but that didn't prevent it having murderous power if need be. The chambers were empty.

'Was it a habit of your husband's to have the gun unloaded?' Garth enquired dryly.

'During the day, yes, in case Derek happened to become too inquisitive. You know what boys are. My husband used to load it every night before he went to bed and unloaded it when he got up. But I haven't the vaguest idea where he put the bullets. I suppose I could search . . . '

'No, no, Mrs. Collins, never mind.' Garth rose to his feet, amiability returned to his hollowed face. He put the gun in a big cellophane envelope and gave it to Whittaker.

'I've put you to enough trouble as it is, and we have to be getting back to the Yard right away — oh, just one more thing. You said your husband walked to his office every day. Have you any idea which route he took?'

'Yes, I know it like the palm of my hand. As I told you, he made a ritual of his walk to the office, leaving here at exactly ten past eight and arriving at his office at nine.' Beatrice Collins gestured towards the window. 'He would go down the street outside to the right, turn the corner to the left, and follow Barraclough Street for about three miles — that's where the buses run, you know — then sharp left down Mercer Avenue, through Back Mercer Street, which is a quiet little alley, and so finally into Terancy Street. The whole trip always took him about fifty minutes, so he said.'

Whittaker noted the street names down as she spoke. Then the chief inspector buttoned his coat in obvious preparation for departure.

'Thank you, Mrs. Collins. You've been a far bigger help to us with your statements than you realize. I'll look forward to seeing you with the boy tonight at my office.'

Garth led the way down the path to the car. Without commenting Whittaker eased his long frame under the steering wheel and began to drive back to Scotland Yard.

8

At length Garth and Whittaker were back in the grey austerity of Scotland Yard. It was half past three as they entered the office. Garth took the .38 from Whittaker and locked it in the desk drawer along with the wallet and bunch of keys, then after throwing his hat up on the peg he went over to the interphone.

'Anybody waiting for me?' he asked.

There was — and it materialized presently as Mason, accompanied by a shortish man in a neat dark suit with a look of bewildered indignation on his young, clean-shaven face.

'This is Mr. Howard Farrow, sir,' Mason explained. 'I had him wait for you . . . He was near Amberly Building in Terancy Street this morning. You detailed Boardman and me — '

'So I did! How are you, Mr. Farrow? Do take a seat.' Garth was all geniality and handshake.

Howard Farrow sat down grudgingly.

Mason went out and Whittaker went to his table by the window and set his notebook in front of him.

'Now, sir, all I want is an interview with you . . . Murder is a serious business, you know.'

'Murder!' Howard Farrow's eyes opened very wide.

Garth stumped the end of his cheroot in the ashtray. 'I suppose you weren't informed — ? All right, I'll rectify that. A man was murdered in Amberly Building in Terancy Street this morning, and the only individual observed near the building in what might be called suspicious circumstances, was you. As a matter of fact you were seen by the janitor.'

'No law against looking at a building, is there?' Howard Farrow asked sourly.

'You did more than that, Mr. Farrow. You took notes. In the interests of the case I had to have you located.'

Howard Farrow hesitated for a long moment, then suddenly his truculence seemed to evaporate. He even grinned. Feeling in his breast pocket he handed over a card. Garth took it and repeated the words slowly —

'Howard Farrow, Office of the Surveyor, Metropolitan Area. A surveyor!' Garth looked up sharply.

'That's right. I'm not exactly a surveyor, I'm in the Metropolitan Surveyor's Department. The property around Terancy Street is very old, as you may know. It is — confidentially — condemned. I was simply studying the layout for a new building plan we have in mind. You can check it with my chief if you wish.'

Garth held the card edgewise and grinned blandly. 'Why should I, Mr. Farrow? All right — so you were studying the building . . . Logical! But why so early on as eight-fifteen?'

'Oh, that's simple. I was told to make the survey before going to the office this morning — on my way from home that is. I had a lot of inspecting to do so I started off early, arriving at the office somewhere around ten o'clock.'

'Mmmm . . . ' Garth sat back in his chair. 'A lot of inspecting, you say?

Maybe you can help me, then. Did you, in the course of your activities, happen to see anybody in — or near — Amberly Building?'

'Well,' Howard Farrow reflected, 'something rather odd come to think of it — but it wasn't near Amberly Building.'

Garth moved his hands impatiently. 'Providing it wasn't too distant I'm still interested. What was this — occurrence?'

'It was somebody on a roof overlooking Back Mercer Street, which buildings were included in my inventory of condemned property,' Howard Farrow explained. 'I had gone inside one of the buildings that back on to Back Mercer Street to finish looking round. Then I went up on the roof for a further survey. I'd just commenced it when I caught sight of somebody on a roof — a much lower roof than the one I was on. It was across Back Mercer Street and quite some distance away from me. This person was apparently fiddling with the parapet. Then the person went quickly across the roof to a fire escape ladder and I didn't see anything more of him — or her.'

'Her?' Garth straightened up. 'Some doubt in your mind?'

'Yes. I couldn't tell for certain whether it was a man or a woman, and naturally I'd no reason to try and find out. I thought it was probably an office worker doing something on the roof. It was either a small man or a woman. I saw a dark beret, a blue raincoat with a belt round it, and I think I saw the bottom of dark trousers. But they could have been slacks if it was a woman on a roof excursion.'

'And this fiddling with the parapet business?' Garth questioned. 'What exactly do you mean by that?'

'He or she was doing something to the flat stonework that runs along the edge of the roof. I don't know what, but it didn't take long.'

'And what time did you see all this?'

'It would be about ten to nine I should think.'

'And could you see into Back Mercer Street itself?'

'Er — no. I was too far away for that.'

There was a long pause and then a rustle of paper as Whittaker turned a leaf

110

of his notebook and waited. That earlier sense of ghostliness was absent now. There seemed to be a concrete avenue of investigation opening up.

'You didn't,' Garth asked, edging forward a little, 'hear anything, like — say, a revolver shot?'

Farrow shook his head. 'Nothing like that, inspector. In fact the whole incident probably doesn't mean a thing — '

'This building,' Garth interrupted him, pondering. 'You say it directly overlooks Back Mercer Street?'

'Yes. I think it's the roof of a disused garage or something. If you want to find it, it's the lowest building in that street. In fact Back Mercer Street is only an entry really, connecting with Terancy Street at one end and Ball Street at the other.'

'Splendid!' Garth rose, smiling. 'I'm glad you have been so helpful, Mr. Farrow. Thanks very much. And I'm sorry to have inconvenienced you.'

Farrow looked mollified as he got to his feet.

'Oh that's all right. I didn't realise at

first how serious the matter was. The man who located me and said you wanted an interview with me shouldn't have been so secretive.'

'It runs in policemen,' Garth told him dryly; and then showed him out. Coming back to the desk he stood thinking.

Whittaker closed his notebook emphatically. 'Back Mercer Street, sir? The figure of a small man or else a woman? I'll take a bet it was Mrs. Beatrice Collins.'

'Will you? Haven't you forgotten Collins died in his office?'

'Yes — apparently. We've yet to get the report through that he did, and until then —'

He broke off as following a knock on the door an overalled clerk entered, reports and photographic prints gripped in his hand.

'For you, sir,' he said briefly. 'They just came through — concerning Collins.'

Garth nodded and went round to his swivel chair at the desk. The clerk went out and Whittaker came round to look over his superior's shoulder. Garth picked up the fingerprint record first and read it carefully . . .

Fingerprints Report (Granville Collins Dec'd): Fingerprints in Collins's office are of two varieties, one exceptional arch, 9-ridge, and the other whorl, 10-ridge. The former prints are those of Collins and the latter tally identically with some of those on the tumbler submitted for inspection . . . Prints on five matchboxes are too blurred for examination. It is obvious the boxes have been handled freely.

Rider Forensic Laboratory Report on Matchboxes: These boxes contain minute traces of scale-like substance, pollen grains, phosphorus, and tobacco dust, the usual concomitant of any man's pocket in summer time.

'That's a help,' Garth growled, putting the report on one side and picking up another one.

Footprints Report (G. Collins Dec'd): Many footprints presumably made by the deceased since the size matches his shoes. Also several woman's footprints, particularly prolific under small desk and in front of safe. Photo-enlargements attached.

'Or more plainly, Mary Baxter,' Whittaker commented.

Garth picked up the last of the reports.

Post Mortem Report: Deceased was killed by one bullet from a .38 revolver. The bullet entered just below the pulmonary veins area and after pursuing a slightly erratic course — as many bullets do inside a body — pierced the top of the heart. Judging from its position the bullet must have stopped the heart's action instantaneously. The shot was fired from a distance of roughly fifteen feet. This is open to question, however, as actually it is only possible to judge when a shot has been fired from very far or very near. In between these extremes much is guesswork. Without doubt the shot was fired from a vertical position, evidenced by the shape of the wound, it being oval. Being a direct heart wound blood loss would be almost negligible. Blood very rarely flows copiously from a direct heart wound. Bullet submitted to Firearms for inspection upon your further instructions.

To Chief Inspector Garth.

Garth put the report aside and looked up slowly to meet Whittaker's wide, astonished eyes.

'According to this report Collins died *instantaneously*, sir! That means he was shot in his office, and we've not the vaguest hint of anybody ever having been near him in order to commit the murder!'

9

They returned to Scotland Yard in twelve minutes and the .38 was handed over to 'Dabs' with instructions to pass it on to Firearms afterwards. To this was added the order to have it traced from its number — then, earlier than the appointment had stipulated, Mrs. Collins arrived with her son.

Garth greeted her genially enough as she was shown into the office. 'Have a chair, won't you, Mrs. Collins? You too, son.'

Beatrice Collins seated herself and from his own corner of the office, Sergeant Whittaker could not help noticing how smart she looked, even in black. It confirmed his opinion that she put her personal advancement and appearance above everything.

Most of Garth's concentration seemed to be on the boy Derek, dark-haired like his mother, with something of her

116

smallness of features, but with a sullen look about the mouth that was certainly not hers, nor perhaps even of his father. It was born of his own nature.

'You, young man, are the chap I want to see,' Garth smiled, clapping the boy on the shoulder. He drew up a chair for him at the desk. 'Now, son, this won't take long. You've probably homework to do — same as I have — so we won't waste time, eh?'

'No, sir,' the boy muttered.

Garth's pale eyes switched to the woman's intent but passive face. 'You've acquainted him with the facts, madam?' he asked, and she nodded slowly.

'Good! In that case — ' Garth reflected for a moment, massaging his chest, 'suppose we try and find out why your father was so cross with you this morning, eh, Derek?'

'It was because I slept late, sir,' the boy answered, shrugging.

'But surely, lad, you've overslept before without any rumpus? I understand so from your mother.'

'Dad just happened to be — be extra

cross this morning.'

Garth pulled up a chair and settled on it, leaned towards the boy confidentially. 'Now look here, son, I don't want you to think of me as a big bad policeman. I'm talking to you as man to man. Your father has been murdered. You know that.'

Derek Collins shied away from the cold, staring eyes and found relief in looking at the desk. 'Yes, I know,' he admitted quietly.

'And you must want to help the police find out who did it . . . '

'Yes, sir. But — ' The boy stared at Garth defiantly for a moment. 'Honest, mister, I don't know anything about who — who killed my father! It had nothing to do with my sleeping late, anyway.'

'No; but it may have had something to do with something else! Look at me, son. Are you absolutely sure that your father only quarrelled with you because you overslept? Was that the *only* reason?'

Garth's pale coloured eyes were like those of a snake.

'Or did your father find you up to something? Something which to you might have seemed ordinary enough but which to him might have appeared as something quite criminal?'

The boy had gone visibly pale but he still kept shaking his head stubbornly. 'There wasn't anything else. Honest!'

Garth kept his eyes fixed on him. 'Son, do you collect matchboxes?'

Mrs. Collins looked vaguely surprised and the boy jerked his head up again. 'No, I don't collect 'em — not really,' he said.

'But you have seen them lying about the house now and again, and on such occasions picked them up and kept them — in your bedroom perhaps, or in some drawer — like I did when I was a kid?'

Garth was grinning again. Slightly reassured by the change in mood the boy nodded.

'Yes, sir, I've done that many a time, but what's that got to do with my dad being . . . being — ?'

'Were you fond of your father?' Garth asked suddenly.

'I suppose so,' Derek muttered.

'Well, let's say — did you respect him?

Enough to obey his orders without ever thinking of disobeying?'

'Oh yes, sir! I would never have dared to disobey dad once he gave an order.'

A look of revelation passed over Garth's features. 'Know anything about air-rifles, son?'

'A bit,' Derek said. 'One of the older boys in my school has a B.S.A. air-rifle — a real beauty. He lets me fire it now and again but I'm not a very good shot and — ' Conscious of having been led into unexpected fields the boy added wonderingly, 'Why?'

'Oh, I just wondered if you are the same as I was when a boy,' Garth replied, shrugging. Then: 'Which school do you go to?'

'Midstone Grammar,' Mrs. Collins said, her voice oddly hard. 'It's rather a distance from home but the best one available . . . '

'And this morning, after all the rumpus about oversleeping were you in time for school or not?' Garth asked.

Derek hesitated. 'I — er — I was a bit late, that's all.'

'Look here Inspector, just what are you getting at?' Beatrice Collins asked curtly, clearly angry. 'Derek has not done anything: why should he be subjected to a cross examination in this fashion? Why don't you tackle an adult, like me for instance?'

'Because, madam, I find adults singularly evasive sometimes — unlike children,' Garth smiled grimly as his eyes bored at her.

'That's no answer!' She got to her feet impatiently. 'And I'm rather tired of this questioning and nonsense. Good heavens, Mr. Garth, one would think I was the guilty person instead of the bereaved! There is a limit, you know!'

'I see that your nerves are a little tried, Mrs. Collins, and I don't blame you,' Garth said amiably as he strolled to the door and opened it. 'Suppose we leave things as they are for the moment, eh? And thank you so much for coming — and you, too, lad. Mind you don't hurt anybody with that air-rifle or I'll be after you.'

'Yes, sir.' The boy looked doubtful as

his mother whirled him out of the office. Garth closed the door on them slowly and returned to the desk.

'Why — an air-rifle?' Whittaker asked, closing his notebook.

'Why not?' Garth settled back at his desk. 'You see, Whitty, it's just as well to have a line on the boy and his activities — chiefly because he's lying. That 'oversleeping' eyewash wouldn't fool a baby. Collins wasn't so unbalanced as to fly into a mad rage just because the boy was asleep, particularly as it had happened before and he'd never said anything then, if Mrs. Collins is to be believed. There is much more than *that* behind it. Something so deep that that boy now hates his father, or rather his father's memory. And why? Probably because what seemed a crime to the father seems quite a natural thing to the boy. There is no greater offence to a child mind than to be outrageously attacked for something that, to the child, seems innocent. The memory remains — deep-seated.'

'This sounds as though we're getting

into psychiatry, sir,' Whittaker commented.

'Maybe we are.' Garth reflected. 'In time I'll make sure. Back of my mind I'm beginning to fit into place all the odd little facets in Collins's character, but I've got to think them out. My question about air-rifles was simply to see if the lad might have a knowledge of how firearms work. It is inconceivable that he could not have seen that gun which his father kept in his room. Therefore, knowing the principles of an air-rifle, he must know how to fire a revolver.'

'Great Scott, sir, you don't think *he* did it!'

'I cannot afford to ignore the possibility. There is motive, remember — bitter resentment against his father. On the other side of the scales we have to weigh the typewritten note. Just assessing possibilities, Whitty, that's all.'

Garth reached for the telephone and raised it. 'Get me Midstone Grammar School,' he ordered. He sat waiting, his eyes aimed at the ceiling. Whittaker frowned, browsing through the notes he had made during the long day. That suggestion of the ghost still paraded. Mrs. Collins and her son both had motive, and the woman's alibi was a weak one. As for the boy, he had been at school and —

'Midstone Grammar School?' Garth asked suddenly. 'Could I speak to the Principal? Right . . . ' There was a pause as the pendulum of the office wall clock swung busily. The time was six twenty.

'Hello — ! The Principal? Dr. Everton — ? This is Scotland Yard, C.I.D. — Chief Inspector Garth speaking. Sorry to bother you but I've a little checking to do. You have a pupil on your register by the name of Derek Collins — Pardon? Yes, you'll have seen the preliminary announcement in the papers, I suppose? The son of Granville Collins, yes . . . All I want to know is did Derek Collins attend school this morning, and if so at what time. Yes, I'll wait . . . '

Garth looked at his blotter pensively as he waited. Then:

'I see,' he said slowly. 'Thanks very much, Doctor. Goodbye.' He dropped the telephone to its cradle and swung round

124

in his chair to face the sergeant.

'Derek Collins did not go to school this morning,' he announced. 'This afternoon, yes — but not this morning. So what do you make of that?'

10

Sergeant Whittaker was incredulous. 'It sounds as if you are trying to prove that Derek Collins has no alibi — that he could have been just anywhere when his father met his death! Well, I refuse to regard it as logical that a twelve-year-old boy would, or even could, kill his own father.'

'If you look through the crime records, Whitty, you'll find plenty of cases where boys of twelve, and younger — and girls too occasionally, bless 'em! — have committed murder with guns, with even less provocation than Derek seems to have had . . . but I too am something of a logician,' he went on dryly. 'There are too many irreconcilable points against it. The note, for one thing, death in the office for another, attire of the person seen by Howard Farrow for another. Where would Derek get a beret from, I wonder? No — that isn't my reason for checking on the boy. It was to see if he had played truant, and if there was yet another reason for him holding back information . . . '

Whittaker gave a savage rub at his hair. 'What's the fact of Derek not going to school this morning got to do with it? As far as I can see it simply proves that he could have murdered his father in the time, even though dozens of facts are against it.'

'It also proves this, my feet-on-the-earth friend.' Garth tapped his finger on the desk. 'His father caught him up to something and swore what he would do for him if he ever caught him at it again. That something, I'm convinced, was not over-sleeping! On top of that he plays truant from school. The reasoning there is that if he admits one thing — when ordered not to do so by his father — he may find that his school truancy, a serious offence to a schoolboy, will be found out — so he keeps stolidly quiet about everything to make sure. That's the way it works. I know, dammit. I've two daughters and a son of my own as examples.'

'It's cockeyed,' Whittaker commented, after reflection.

'To you and me — yes. To a boy of twelve — not by a long shot! Get smart! Don't admit one thing and they'll discover nothing. The lad's scared out of his wits. It is either the fear of his truancy being discovered which keeps him quiet, or else a loyalty to the promise he made his father. This latter view I don't quite agree with, but it is possible.'

'Then what happens, sir? The boy will never speak!'

Garth grinned widely. 'He'll speak the next time because I'll have my at present cloudy theory fully in focus by then, I hope. I intend to show him why he collects old matchboxes. If I have the hang of this thing properly the matchbox angle is the simplest in the whole case. It's that instantaneous death which has me worried. It kicks the props from under every other notion I've conceived.'

'Matchboxes . . . ' Whittaker mused. 'Just what have they got to do with it?'

Garth got to his feet. 'No statement without proof, Whitty. That's me. Besides, if you want to earn promotion you'll have to do some reasoning of your own. You can help yourself best by casting back to your boyhood and remembering what you did with matchboxes.'

'I'll sleep on it, sir,' Whittaker decided. 'What's next?'

'I'm going along to see if the boys have finished with that thirty-eight yet.'

Garth left the office. Fingerprints reported that there was no sign of anything on the gun and that it had been passed on to Colonel Fordyce of Firearms. The usual machinery was in motion for checking the registration number.

Garth found Fordyce just preparing to go home after his day's work. A short, ginger-moustached man with eyes as piercing as javelins he nodded genially to Garth as he came in.

'You found it, Garth,' he said briefly. 'That gun fired the bullet which settled Collins's earthly account. There are five bullets left and the gun barrel is still foul. Not long since it was discharged.'

'Thanks, Colonel,' Garth beamed. 'There's a question I'd like to ask. Do you think a boy of twelve, somewhat big for his age, could fire a thirty-eight with unerring accuracy straight to the heart?'

Colonel Fordyce buttoned his suit coat meticulously and thought the question out. 'From what distance?'

'According to Doc Myers's report — fifteen feet.'

Fordyce grinned cynically at a passing thought. 'Yes, I should think it is possible as far as physique is concerned. What I have against it is the mental control. I don't believe any boy of twelve would be sufficiently calm and steady to fire a revolver, and a thirty-eight at that, straight to the heart — unless of course the gun were resting on something. Freehand, I'd say it could not be done.'

'Mmmm — thanks,' Garth turned to go.

'Just a moment, Garth! Fifteen feet, you say? Doc Myers should keep within his own province. He's guessing! You can't tell exactly how far a shot comes from. You can tell in which *direction* by the track of the bullet, of course, but even that is not always accurate because of bone and tissue resistance. Fifteen feet!'

Fordyce shook his head. 'More than I'd like to swear to.'

'I know,' Garth answered grinning. 'Dr. Myers has been guessing, and I know it, but I think he made a guess that isn't very far out. Anyway, I hope not.'

The Colonel nodded and Garth left the room. Back in the office he made matters clear to the puzzled Whittaker.

'Do you still think that lad shot his father, sir?' he asked.

'Frankly, Whitty,' — Garth reached for his hat — 'I don't think anything about it, I'm still checking on angles. Personally I don't think he shot his father or had anything to do with it. Personal opinion apart, the evidence shows that he could have had a good deal to do with it.'

'And no fingerprints on the gun?' Whittaker mused.

'As I told you this afternoon, Whitty, prints on a gun are rare. Even poroscopy stands a better chance than fingerprints. No, I'm leaving the machinations of Derek Collins to jell while I pin other things down in my mind.'

'There's Dudley Morton and his

once-a-month visit, tying up maybe with the thousand pounds a month,' Whittaker remarked hopefully.

'That can wait for a while. Dudley Morton is too important a man in the City to pack up his traps and clear, and for all we know there is no earthly reason why he should. I'll deal with him tomorrow . . . For the moment I'm going home to read this!'

He picked up the book on will power from the desk drawer and jammed it in his pocket.

'I have the feeling it's the answer to part of the problem,' he added, seeing Whittaker's vague look. 'And if it isn't, maybe I'll find out how to hypnotise the wife and prevent her wanting that new hat she's already thinking about . . . '

*　*　*

Arriving back in his office the following morning. Garth found Sergeant Whittaker typing out the shorthand notes of the previous day's statements, while in the hide armchair by the doorway there sat a

132

woman of early middle age, fashionable in a way, with a face which had once been pretty but which was now in a state of decided disrepair.

'Good morning, madam.' Garth nodded to her genially as threw his hat on the peg. 'I haven't the pleasure of — '

'This is Miss Evelyn Drew, sir,' Whittaker explained, rising. 'She wants to see you — personally.'

'Splendid!' Garth, Whittaker noticed, seemed to be in a genial mood as he tugged the book on will power out of his pocket and planked it in the desk drawer. Then he settled himself in the swivel chair.

'You are, of course, Chief Inspector Garth?' the woman asked, her tone challenging.

Garth nodded slowly, studying her impassively. Her eyes were grey and very level, with long black lashes, but the rest of her face was lined, embittered in some indefinable way. Mousy hair sprouted in undisciplined fashion from under a halo hat.

'I read in the papers this morning a

small paragraph about the suspected murder of Mr. Collins. It said you had charge of the case and that any information would be welcomed if it concerned Mr. Collins.'

'And you have some information?' Garth asked hopefully.

'Well — sort of. You see, I worked for Mr. Collins fifteen years ago, when he had only just started in business for himself and was very small fry. I went to him as a clerk. I was of course only a young woman then . . . '

'Naturally,' Garth conceded courteously.

'Granville Collins,' Evelyn Drew said, her voice rising, 'was a *beast*!'

Whittaker cleared his throat and looked under his eyes at his superior. Garth did not even blink at the woman's observation.

'That, madam, covers a wide field,' he commented, with a faint grin. 'I'd be glad if you'd explain . . . '

'You bet I will! At that time I was twenty-three — ambitious, and more or less innocent. I was pretty too,' she added, with a sulky pride. 'Everything went on all right for a couple of months while I worked for Collins, then he sort of — er — became rather intimate.

'I'm afraid I didn't repel him. I was young and pretty inexperienced — and I liked him then. He was tall, good looking, altogether attractive. And I didn't know until afterwards that he was married. He never told me. I thought I was on to a good thing. I freely admit that I thought he would ask me to marry him.'

There was a significant little hush as the revelations of a new side of the dead man's character were dumped in the spotlight with all the quiet gentility of a load of manure.

'Well, everything seemed to be going fine,' Evelyn Drew went on fiercely. 'Then it occurred to me that we'd never been out anywhere together . . . One day I suggested a theatre, rather a poky one as it was in those days, but it had a first class revue show every week. And what do you think he did?'

Garth leaned across the desk, his face grim. 'He probably told you to go to hell, madam.'

'Yes!' Her voice was going uphill again. 'Yes, that's just what he *did* say! More than that — he fired me on the spot! Gave me a month's wages in lieu of notice and told me to get out and never come back . . . But how on earth did *you* know?'

Garth gave a hard grin. 'And fired you as well, eh? Well, that's logical too . . . '

'Logical!' The woman jumped up from the armchair and thumped the desk. 'It *wasn't* logical, and for fifteen years I've wondered why in the world he did it. At the time I was so astonished at his reaction to a perfectly normal suggestion I couldn't sort of think straight. Then later on, when I learned in roundabout ways that he was married, I tumbled to it. He didn't want to be seen in a theatre with me in case his wife happened to get to know of it.'

'Mmmm,' Garth murmured. 'And that satisfied you?'

'It had to — but I still felt bitter. I had nothing I could take to law or I would have done. I know it's only an incident, Inspector,' Evelyn Drew went on, the challenging note fading out of her voice, 'but Collins treated me rottenly and I've been bursting to tell somebody about it for fifteen years. Now I've done it — when it no longer matters — I feel better.'

'I'm glad you do,' Garth said politely. 'Incidentally, did Collins seem to you to be a man of peculiar habits?'

She flashed him a quick, keen glance.

'Yes — in many ways. For one thing he had an office too big for his business and used to have his desk right in the middle of it — like a postage stamp in the middle of a big table, I used to say. Then he'd let the fire go out before he'd go in the cellar for coal. He wouldn't get his own coat out of the clothes cupboard we had, either. Used to ask me to do it, and if I didn't happen to be in he'd go without it. But all the same I loved him, until he fired me.'

'And then you hated him?'

The faded face set harshly. 'Yes!'

'His office was not in Terancy Street at that time, I presume?'

'No — Bagot Street, some two miles away.'

'I see. And what is your occupation now, Miss Drew?'

'I'm with Thorne and Buxton, the grain people. Pretty good job as chief clerk. I ought to be at my work now, by rights, only I called in to tell you the pretty bits.'

'For which many thanks. Can you tell me what you were doing between, say, eight and nine yesterday morning?'

'I don't see why I should,' she answered calmly. 'And you can't make me. I know my rights. Incidentally, according to the judges' rules, oughtn't I to sign a statement of what I've just said?'

'You can if it will give you any pleasure,' Garth replied shrugging. 'Since you are not being accused — '

'Never mind, I don't want it.' She smiled cynically. 'I'm merely showing you that I know what I'm doing.'

'Of that, I was never in doubt, madam.' Garth got up and opened the door for her. 'Thank you so much, Miss Drew. Good morning.'

She nodded a farewell and Garth closed the door upon her.

'Pretty story,' Whittaker said, finishing

his notes on the interview. 'Though I can understand it. At twenty-three she was probably a looker. Wonder why some women fade so ingloriously?'

'At least she was delightfully frank about it all,' Garth commented.

'You believe her, sir?'

'Why shouldn't I? I believe her because she really is stones lighter after getting that unsavoury fifteen-year old incident off her sagging bosom. You realise that she has done something for us, too, in regard to Collins?'

Whittaker nodded. 'She's shown us that he was a bit of a lad when he was younger.'

'I'd be more inclined to say immoral — even unscrupulous. We must remember that. It may help. If he was like that as a young man, and his wife has testified that he was intolerable as a much older man, it is possible that his unpleasantness was also too much for the person who murdered him ... Hmmm — fifteen years. Long while. He must have carried on his business in the meantime before the advent of Mary Baxter six months ago. Collins had apparently got over his flighty moments with young women, if Mary Baxter is to be believed.'

'Maybe he worked on his own, sir?' Whittaker said.

'Unlikely. I imagine he perhaps had quite a few clerks working for him at different times but that they're saying nothing for fear of getting exposed in an unfavourable light, despite my request, through the press, for information. Well, it doesn't much matter. I think I know enough about Collins now to satisfy myself what was wrong with him.'

'Incidentally,' Whittaker said, 'how *did* you know he told that Drew woman to go to hell?'

Garth grinned. 'As I said to her, it was quite logical — knowing what I do now about Collins. I've read that book on will power, and done a lot of hard thinking besides. I'll tell you about that later on. Can't now because Dudley Morton is due any moment.'

A blank look crossed Whittaker's face.

'I called at his office on the way here — it's quite near Throgmorton Street. In fact it is one of the distant buildings we could see from that flat roof in Back Mercer Street. I left a message for him, pre-written at home in a confidential envelope of course, and asked him to drop in here for a chat. That gent interests me quite a lot.'

Whittaker nodded, then went back to his table in the corner. For quite ten minutes he was busy at the noiseless typewriter — ten minutes in which Garth spent his time writing down short lines on his scratch-pad and numbering them as he went. Once, as he had to cross the office, Whittaker caught a glimpse of them and did a spot of private musing to himself.

1. *Avoided small washroom.*
2. *Ran down narrow passage.*
3. *Avoided theatres and cinemas.*
4. *Bedroom to self.*
5. *Disliked clothes in cupboard.*
6. *Postage stamp on table top simile.*
7. *Five matchboxes.*

This was as far as Garth had got when there was a knock on the door. He covered the sheet hastily and took his cheroot from his mouth.

Whittaker got up as a constable admitted a slender, clean-shaven, small-shouldered man of about fifty-five, immaculately dressed in grey. He was perhaps five feet four in height, with hair of a fascinating colour of rich silver blonde, thick and wavy and parted on the left-hand side.

11

'Inspector Garth?' the visitor asked, coming into the office.

Garth nodded amiably and got up, shook the hand extended to him. 'Morning, Mr. Morton. Good of you to come along. I know you must be a busy man.'

'Oh, forget that, Inspector! I gathered from your note you wished to see me about Collins? I expected it, really, after reading in the morning papers about his death.'

Garth nodded to a chair and Dudley Morton seated himself crossing perfectly trousered legs. He was a quiet spoken man of obvious refinement, good looking after a fashion. His eyes were grey and friendly, his nose straight. His mouth spoiled him. Apart from it being filled with uncannily white screw-in type of teeth, the upper lip was too long and the lower lip too short. It made him look as though he were incessantly biting something. Whittaker for his part tried to imagine whether the man was silver-haired or a natural platinum blonde.

For some reason, ever since Morton had come into the office, Garth had been looking at the stockbroker's right ear — not pointedly or even noticeably, but Whittaker had observed the interest and now hovered over his notebook again.

'Perhaps,' Garth said finally, 'it would be best if I let you talk in your own way, Mr. Morton — at least to begin with. I'm anxious to find out all I can about Granville Collins.'

Dudley Morton nodded easily. 'He was one of my best friends, Mr. Garth. I knew a lot about him — and there are few men I have admired so much. He was a brilliant businessman with a phenomenal skill in foreseeing the markets — but apart from that he was grand company socially. He had imagination and in practically every subject we discussed he always seemed to see eye to eye with me.'

'Did he, though?' Garth commented, somewhat dryly. 'You didn't find him eccentric in any way?'

'Good heavens, no!' Morton laughed. 'He had foibles, of course . . . in little things, but which of us hasn't?'

'You visited him once a month in his new offices, I believe? In Terancy Street, which he took over about last Christmas?'

'Yes, that's right,' Morton said promptly. 'I suppose you found out about that from his clerk, Miss Baxter?'

'Uh-huh. I'm also wondering if the sum of one thousand pounds paid to Collins once a month and transferred by him to his bank about the third of each month had anything to do with you? It is rather a coincidence.'

'I can soon clear that up.' Morton felt at his pockets for a moment and Garth extended the cigarette box from the desk.

The broker nodded his thanks, lit up, then sat back comfortably. 'Yes, Mr. Garth, I paid Granville Collins that money every month for fifteen years, and I was glad to do it.'

'Really?' Garth smiled blandly. 'I'd need very good results if I paid anybody that amount!'

'With Collins you'd have had them! Two-fifty a week is trifling when you can make thousands with the knowledge it buys. Collins was a genius at foreseeing the up and down movement of Share speculations. Eighty times out of a hundred he guessed rightly which way the market would go, and I paid him that money every month as a sort of retainer fee. He was satisfied, and so was I. Whenever a hot tip was going round I was the first to know of it — and cashed in.'

Every word that had been spoken by Dudley Morton fitted into its allotted place and an onlooker would have said that the statements were quite natural. Yet Whittaker felt uneasy. As for Garth he simply smiled disarmingly.

'Well, then, so you paid him a retainer fee, eh? That clears up a lot of my worries. But, Mr. Morton, tell me, you are a stockbroker in a big way: you are well-known in the City. Even I have heard of you . . . ' Garth did not elaborate on how much he had heard. 'Collins, on the other hand, as I know from various sources, was by no means in a big way

— compared to you that is — and fifteen years ago he was in even less of a big way. Yet you came to him for advice. Y'know, it reminds me of a Regius Professor of Mathematics asking a first-former what twice two is . . . '

Dudley Morton tapped grey dust into the ashtray. 'Quite simply, Inspector, Collins had a gift for foreseeing the markets which I do not possess.'

'But if he had that why didn't he make a fortune for himself? He didn't, you know: I've checked up on that.'

'You do not suggest, Inspector, that I should explain the private monetary affairs of Granville Collins, do you? I have told you why I paid him a thousand pounds a month. There, as I see it, my responsibility ends.' There was, for a moment, a suggestion of fanged teeth behind the quiet voice. Garth sensed it.

'I'm just a policeman, Mr. Morton. I have to ask awkward questions — and you with your one thousand a month have put yourself right in line for about the most awkward batch of questions of all. Anyway, for routine's sake, what were you doing between eight and nine yesterday morning?'

'Er — ' Morton paused and Garth waited patiently, his cold gaze straying again to Morton's ear and then back to the placid face. Suddenly the broker seemed to remember. 'Why yes, of course! I was talking to my wife! On the 'phone.'

'Uh-huh. For how long?'

'Quite fifteen minutes I should think. The rest of the time I was getting to my office.'

'I take it you are very devoted?'

'This,' Dudley Morton said grimly, 'was important business. Let me explain; I left home in my car at eight-thirty, as I always do, and got to my office about twenty to nine. My staff arrives at eight-thirty, chiefly because there is a good deal of preliminary to go through before we officially open at nine. At quarter to nine my wife rang me up with the details of an important letter that had just arrived through the mail. The mail was late yesterday morning: usually it comes before I leave home. She read me these details, stock numbers and so on, over the 'phone. I had my switchgirl make an auxiliary contact to a Dictaphone, as a matter of fact, so the conversation could be transcribed later on.'

'I see.' Garth was blandly genial as he looked at the stockbroker again. 'I hope you won't take offence at all this probing, Mr. Morton: it happens to be for your good as much as ours. I'll come with you to the office and check up, if you don't mind.'

Morton got to his feet, picked up his grey trilby hat. 'By all means. I hardly expected you to take my word for it.'

Garth reached out to the scratchpad and scribbled a brief note, handed it across to Whittaker.

'Get that typed, Whitty, along with the reports while I'm gone. Shan't be long . . . '

Whittaker read the note — *Check on postal deliveries to Morton's home yesterday morning* — and then turned back to his desk. Beaming, Garth pulled his hat from the peg and accompanied the stockbroker downstairs to the Daimler outside.

'I suppose,' Morton said, reflecting as an impassive chauffeur drove them through the traffic, 'it is rather unfortunate for me that poor Collins's office happened to be so close to mine?'

Garth looked out of the window. 'How so?'

'Well, I can see Amberly Building from my private office window, you know — across the roofs. That must make you suspect me more than anybody else. Right in sight of the place.'

'That doesn't prove a thing, sir,' Garth answered quietly. 'In fact it is of no more interest to me than the fact that it is also within view of Back Mercer Street. Most of the buildings in the financial world huddle together in a given area. No significant point in that.'

'I don't want to sound novelettish, Inspector, but have you found any — clues?'

Garth grinned. 'Clues don't hang from trees ready for dumb detectives to pluck down. There are certain pointers, of course, but since none of them make sense as yet there wouldn't be much point

150

in telling you what they are.'

Morton smiled rather ruefully. 'No; of course not.'

Before long the chauffeur stopped the car outside Morton's business premises and the broker led the way into the general office. There was an air of industry about the place, men and women moving in various directions on appointed errands. Beyond muttering 'good mornings' as he swept through the midst of them to the door of his private office Morton took no notice of the dutiful greetings aimed at him.

The private office was sumptuous, all dark oak panelling, rich carpet, metal filing cabinets, and a monstrous shining flat-topped desk. The chairs were of the tubular variety with red hide seats. Garth declined one as Morton offered it and instead went across to the broad windows. Silent, he gazed out over a huddle of low roofs towards the distant old-fashioned lighthouse of a building that was obviously Amberly Building.

Morton nodded through the window. 'If I were an athlete, which I'm not, I could leave my office by this window, hurry across the roofs, and so to Amberly Building.'

'To kill your best friend?' Garth asked calmly.

'I offer it purely as a suggestion, Inspector.'

'Then I'm afraid it doesn't interest me. I imagine that if you had wanted to kill your best friend you'd think of something far less acrobatic and infinitely more subtle.'

Morton smiled with his top lip, revealing those intensely white teeth. 'Whom would you like to speak to first, Inspector?'

'The switchgirl, please.'

The broker nodded and crossing to the interphone summoned the girl to his office. She came in presently, a short, dark-haired creature with a very long nose and a mathematical forehead.

'This is Chief Inspector Garth of Scotland Yard, Miss Hodder,' Morton explained, with a touch of cynicism. 'He has a few questions for you.'

'Scotland Yard?' The girl looked startled. 'But what have I done? I — '

'Relax, Miss Hodder,' Garth told her, smiling. 'This won't take a moment. Yesterday morning Mr. Morton had a telephone call from his home — his wife I believe?' And as the girl nodded: 'At what time?'

'I have it accurately on my check-sheet, but off-hand I'd say it was about eight forty-five. Then Mr. Morton asked me to plug in right away to the Dictaphone so the conversation could be recorded.'

'Mmmm . . . Was Mrs. Morton interrupted while she gave these details?'

'Yes — quite a few times. Mr. Morton asked her to go back over certain points to make sure of them.'

'And it lasted about fifteen minutes?'

'A trifle longer. I think it was eighteen.'

Garth nodded, indicating he had finished. The girl gave her employer a puzzled glance and left the office.

'Is there anybody else you would like to speak to, Inspector?'

'Er — no, I think not.' Garth dug his hands in his pockets. 'I haven't the right to ask you this, Mr. Morton, and you are perfectly entitled to refuse, but there are

153

two things I would like to have done.'

Morton shrugged. 'Name them. I'll help if I can.'

'I'd like the actual recording from the Dictaphone for examination by our analysts, and I also want a typist to type out 'A quick movement of the enemy would jeopardize six gunboats' on *each* of the five machines you have in the outer office. I noticed them as I came in.'

Morton gave a half regretful smile.

'And if I refuse I suppose you'll get at me some other way?'

Garth smiled coldly. 'I'm afraid the Yard doesn't accept refusals when something is needed.'

'Well, you can have the recording with pleasure, but I am puzzled by the request for typing. You want specimens of the machines, I take it. Why?'

'Because somebody knew Collins was going to die and sent a typewritten warning to that effect.'

'Really? But you surely don't think that if I had anything to do with the murder I'd have used one of the office machines for the note?'

'No; I credit you with more sense. But you don't know the private lives of all your employees, do you? One of them might have had a grudge, might have sent the note . . .'

'I see. You're very thorough, aren't you? But you missed a machine. I have this one here.'

Morton turned to a shining oak-topped table by the window. A touch on a treadle-like lever turned the top over and a brand new machine bobbed up and became level. The broker waved a hand to it and picked up a blank memorandum sheet from the bigger desk.

'Here you are, Inspector — type your doggerel while I instruct a clerk to get the recording and test the other machines.'

Garth went over to the machine and squatted down, picked out the line that revealed every character on the machine, as far as the letters were concerned, and half aside he heard Morton issuing his orders through the interphone. Garth was quite aware that the machine he was operating was not the one he sought, but he finished the test line just the same and

155

pushed the paper in his pocket.

The office was quiet again. A big oak clock on a shelf supported by a chromium bracket said it was 10.40; then a girl clerk came in with a small box and a sheet of typing. She eyed Garth somewhat furtively, placed them all on the desk and then went out again.

'All yours, Inspector,' Morton said dryly. 'What happens next?'

Garth picked up the box and put the paper in his pocket. 'To be perfectly frank I am wondering if I could borrow your car to get back to the Yard?'

'By all means. Just tell the chauffeur to drop you wherever you wish . . . ' The stockbroker got to his feet. 'You'll let me know how you get on?'

Garth smiled. 'You can rely on it. Thank you — 'Morning.'

12

Sergeant Whittaker aimed an eager eye at Garth as he came back into the office and placed the recordings on his desk. Garth threw his hat up onto the peg, went over to the Dictaphone in the corner and fitted in a recording. Then, switching it on, he stood listening with Whittaker.

It was as Morton had said: several times he interrupted his wife during the conversation, the conversation itself being a complicated mass of figures, permutations, and the names of shares, stuff which could only have meaning for a stockbroker. At the end of the recording the voice cut off in mid-sentence.

'There was more,' Garth said, turning and nodding to the small box. 'The whole conversation took fifteen minutes, but this is enough for me. I take it as granted that if Morton interrupted his wife on this record he also did it on the others. The switchgirl did all the listening-in and she's to be relied on.'

'Which proves what, sir?'

'I just wondered if Morton had perhaps used the old gag of getting somebody to telephone him and then dashed off from his office while the one-way talk was in progress — his wife being in the know beforehand, of course. In five minutes he could have skedaddled over the roofs to Collins's office and in five minutes he could have got back and nobody been the wiser. But these interruptions kill the idea stone dead . . . or seem to.'

He came back to the desk and took out the two sheets with typewriting upon them, set them down.

'All right! This ends the collecting! Now comes the sifting. From known premises we're going to start hammering the first nails into a killer's coffin . . . First!' He switched on the interphone: 'Ask Dr. Pierce of the radio department to step over to my office, will you?'

Presently Dr. Pierce, tall, bald, and wearing a white smock, came in. He nodded genially, eyes bright behind his thick rimless spectacles.

' 'Morning, Mort! What's on your mind this time?'

'Don't *call* me that! Mortimer — or nothing! Anyway, to get down to it. You can take a record of a voice in light instead of sound, can't you?'

'Certainly we can. It's done every day on sound-film anyway. Photoelectric cell and the electronic vibration of — '

'Okay, don't get technical. I'm a copper not a scientist, but I like to put you chaps with the brains through the hoops now and again. Over there are some Dictaphone recordings with two voices on them. I want you to separate the voices, and record them independently in light.'

Pierce grinned. 'You mean you want separate sound-prints of each voice transferred to transparent sound tape so the voice can be seen as well as heard?'

'That's it! I may never need them anyway. It's just a hunch I'm playing. When you've done it file the voices away. Later I may want you to help me again. Okay?'

'Science at your service,' Pierce assented,

picking the recordings up. 'See you later.'

He nodded and went out. Garth lighted a fresh cheroot and then motioned Whittaker to the desk. The Sergeant placed the almost completed typewritten record of statements down on the blotter.

'Now, let's get things in order,' Garth said. 'First — we have Collins shot in the heart from a vertical direction. For convenience I'll say the shot was fifteen feet away. Either the shot *did* come from above, or he was stooping and received it while in a horizontal position. Right?'

'Right,' Whittaker agreed.

'There was nobody in or near his office who could have fired the shot, yet Calthorpe and Mason and the psychologist Andrew Martin all swear they heard something *like* a shot. I suggest that a *shot* was *not* heard, just something resembling it. The absence of fumes in the office supports my theory that what they actually heard was the window slamming.'

'The window . . . ' Whittaker rolled the word over his tongue like a sweetmeat.

160

'The one under which Collins was found, you mean?'

'Obviously. The other one was jammed with paint. The window I mean is very hard to raise, but it came down like a ton of bricks. You get that with these old fashioned sash windows. Down she comes and —WHAM! When it strikes the bottom of the frame it makes the hell of a din. Mason heard it, so did Martin, so did Calthorpe far away outside. Such a sound resembles a revolver shot and events being as they were, imagination supplied the rest.'

Whittaker nodded excitedly. 'Collins could easily have opened the window — say for fresh air — and somebody shot him from a distance. Still holding the window he fell on the floor and dragged the window shut with him. That would account for no bullet hole in the glass.'

'From where did a shot come?' Garth asked pointedly. 'We know that nobody was outside the building or on the roof or suspended somewhere where they could not be seen. And no buildings overlook Collins's office, remember. On top of

161

which, he was shot from *above*.'

'Or horizontally!'

'With the unseen killer hanging in mid-air directly in front of him? Hardly! And if he were stooping, his breast line would be above window base level anyway.'

Whittaker fell silent. The ghost that had been having the time of its life since Collins had been found was now enjoying a field day.

'What made you think it was the window slamming?' Whittaker asked finally.

'Logic!' Garth grinned round his cheroot. 'Ever since I heard the three statements about a 'sort of bang' and the 'perhaps it was a gun'. If it *had* been a gun no doubt would have been in the minds of Calthorpe and Mason, trained to that sort of thing. Nothing in the office was overturned; the weight of Collins's body falling to the floor couldn't account for the sound — but recalling the startlingly easy way the window dropped when pulled down, after the hard labour of getting it up, I came to the conclusion that only that could account for it. That, and the lack of fumes.'

'But wouldn't Martin have heard it slamming many times before?'

'Not necessarily, if Collins was not in the habit of slamming the window every time he closed it. He only did it this time because he died still holding the window, and his weight slammed it down. Remember how we found him, with hands stretched nearly to the wall.'

'Then for the love of Mike how *was* he shot? As it stands, sir, the thing is impossible!'

Garth smiled sourly. 'It happened! That being so the only thing we can allow to enter into the proceedings is an accident — something utterly unplanned by anybody, which has produced the cumulative effect of an *apparently* impossible crime. Back of my mind is a dim, half-formed idea that perhaps . . . Never mind; it'll have to jell. Besides I must go through some evidence I've seen somewhere. It's sticking at the back of my subconscious mind . . . All right, so we are going to accept the window as the explanation of the 'shot'. Either Collins opened it for fresh air — which I don't believe he did — or else it was for *another* reason which might help us considerably.'

Garth reached for his scratchpad and contemplated it.

'Let's weigh up Collins's peculiar character and see where it gets us. I think I have one answer to a whole lot of puzzling things but let's get Dr. Grimshaw, our pet psychiatrist, to pass judgment. He ought to know.'

He turned to the interphone and his request for Dr. Grimshaw of the Department of Psychiatry brought that small, perky gentleman into the office looking very impatient.

'I hope you realize, Garth, that you've upset me in the middle of an important prognosis of the Fisher case.' He sat down and glared.

'All right,' Garth said, waving a hand to mollify him. 'I'm not interested in Fisher. I just want your opinion to verify my own. Here's the issue. A man is normal in most things, but the following startling foibles are noticeable in his character: one: he avoided a small rathole of a washroom and had his clerk fetch washing water for him. Two: he walked sedately upstairs where there was a high skylight above admitting a modicum of light but *ran* down the narrow dark corridor to his office door.

'Three; he nearly went berserk when asked to go to a theatre or cinema and always refused. Four: he took a large bedroom to himself and left his wife in the room they had formerly both occupied. Five: he would not get his clothes from a cupboard and had his clerk do it for him. Six: he had his desk in the middle of the office so that, according to his clerk, it looked like a postage stamp on the top of a table. Seven: he refused to have a private car or travel by bus and walked four miles from home to office to avoid both. Eight: once when his clerk drew down the blinds before switching on the light he nearly went crazy with fury. Nine: when given a lacquered box in which to keep odds and ends he flew into a rage when the lid was opened. Ten: he'd let a fire go out before going into a cellar for coal. Eleven; he had an office out of all proportion to the needs of his business . . . That's the lot. What's the answer?'

'Pronounced claustrophobia,' Dr. Grimshaw replied. 'I should have thought you could see that.'

'I did see it,' Garth said calmly. 'I wanted you to verify it. It means fear of enclosed spaces, doesn't it?'

'Certainly it does. Anybody who has all those foibles has obviously got the disease badly — and it *is* a disease! Quite a serious disease of the mind, in extreme cases. It goes on increasing until the root cause is exposed and destroyed. The cause might be a childhood incident — perhaps being shut away under the stairs as a punishment, or something like that.'

Grimshaw gave Garth an acid look. 'Anything else?'

'No thanks, Doc. I just wanted the word of an expert.'

With a growl Grimshaw got to his feet and left the office.

'That point being settled,' Garth smiled, 'it brings us, I believe, to the solution of two other points. First: the visit to Andrew Martin was, as Martin himself said, quite genuine. Clearly Collins visited him in the hope that he could perhaps cure him of his mental trouble. When I pressed Martin he said Collins was suffering a generalized fear of this and that and not a fear that somebody might murder him. Right?'

Whittaker turned up Martin's statement and nodded.

'Right, sir, yes — but wouldn't Collins know if he had got claustrophobia?'

'Not necessarily. He simply considered it as a general fear of this and that. Plain nerves! Which brings us to point two: the book on will power. This gave me the first real hint. The chapter most read is the one on 'How to Master Your Fears'. It is therefore obvious, since the book is ten years old, that he had his trouble then — and if we are to believe Miss Drew's statement he had it fifteen years ago too, when he fired her rather than go to a poky theatre with her.

'He obviously found this book a comfort, something on which to fasten his mind. Hence its place of honour in the safe. It was thinking about this and browsing through the chapter on the various ways of mastering fear, then linking them up with every kink in Collins's character, that enabled me to see what was the matter with him.'

'Yes, sir . . . doesn't it seem that it might link up with those five empty matchboxes too? They represent enclosed spaces, don't they? Maybe he found five matchboxes at home and they — ' Whittaker gestured vaguely — 'sort of affected his mind and he took them to the office.'

'And bored holes in 'em?' Garth suggested imperturbably.

Whittaker frowned. 'Anyway, I think they're connected.'

'Oh-ho, they are!' Garth seemed deeply amused by some inner thought for a moment, then the death mask slowly settled back. 'I'll tie the five matchboxes up later, I think, with an extraction of confession from young Derek Collins — probably when he comes home for lunch. For now, let's take the remaining points . . .

'Motive? One: Andrew Martin — apparently none, though he might have had the opportunity to commit the murder. Two: Mary Baxter — she seems to have had less motive or opportunity than anybody. Her alibi is that she overslept. I haven't checked on it yet with her parents, but I can if need be. For the moment I'm believing her. Three: Howard Farrow of the surveyor's office — he seems genuine enough and his alibi of being some distance away can, and will be, checked. Since he saw somebody fiddling with the parapet and we found a gun there I'll credit him with being truthful. Testing of his alibi comes later. Motive: Apparently none. Four: Mrs. Collins — plenty of motive and opportunity too, if we assume the maid was perhaps bribed. Five: Derek Collins — both motive and opportunity, since he played truant. Six: Evelyn Drew — motive perhaps for fifteen-year-old grievance which hadn't died. Whether she had the opportunity or not yesterday morning we can find out from her firm, since she got snooty when I tried to get an alibi out of her. Got those listed down for checking?'

'Including the janitor, sir,' Whittaker said.

'I think we can discount him,' Garth replied, musing. 'So we come to Dudley Morton. And somewhere, Whitty, I have seen that man before!'

'Newspapers, perhaps?'

'No, no — years ago, when he looked different and I was a young shaver in the force and had no indigestion. Happy days! But I remember *that right ear*!'

Whittaker was respectfully silent. He knew that his superior, like Melvin Purvis of the American F.B.I. — the man who arrested John Dillinger by remembering a photograph of his neck — never forgot a physical aberration once he filed it mentally. In that sense his mind was definitely photographic.

Garth made a restless movement. 'It was something with a criminal flavour, as I remember. Faces alter, the physique changes, but certain things like the angles of jaws, the backs of necks, and especially ears, never change except by absolute injury. And I've seen that long narrow lobe and shallow sulcus somewhere before. Maybe I'll have a look what 'Crow' has to say. Must be fifteen years ago . . . Anyway, let's get back to the man himself. What do you think of him?'

'Not much,' Whittaker replied refreshingly. 'A bit slimy, and I didn't think much of his retainer fee angle, either. As you pointed out, if Collins were that smart why didn't he make a fortune for himself?'

'Lies — all of it,' Garth acknowledged. 'I recall Miss Drew's statement that fifteen years ago Collins was only 'very small fry'. Would the lordly Morton, who was established fifteen years ago, according to the business records I looked up at home, condescend to pay a nobody-stockbroker two-fifty pounds a week for his knowledge? Like hell! I've one guess for the real reason . . . '

'Hush money,' Whittaker said.

'That's it, Whitty. Hush money — blackmail. But that only gets us half way, and it still remains an assumption until we know the reason for blackmail.'

'What about that press cutting we found concerning blackmail? A connection, don't you think?'

'Perhaps; but I'm more inclined to think Collins might have kept that to see how the counsel for the defence arranged his case to get the blackmailer acquitted. Maybe Collins was going to use it as a specimen idea if he ever got landed for blackmail himself.'

'Yes,' Whittaker agreed, surprised. 'I didn't think of that. Anyway, when we know the reason for blackmail we'll be well on the high road.'

'We'll have made a start, anyway,' Garth admitted guardedly. 'Whilst I mull over my notion of having met Morton before somewhere, let's see what we have on him at the present time. He was, with singular convenience, talking over the 'phone to his wife about the time Collins died, or at any rate just before it. The document in question arrived by the mail that morning — late. Did you check on the postal people?'

'They're ringing us back,' Whittaker said.

'Mmmm ... then let's turn to something else.' Garth picked up the original warning note from his desk drawer and spent a moment or two studying it by comparison with the typing specimens he had collected. Finally he shrugged.

'They don't seem to resemble this typing,' he said, 'but that's for the experts to decide. Take this lot in to the Calligraphy Department, Whitty, and tell 'em I want that note checked, cross-checked, fingerprinted — every darned thing. I've got to know what machine typed it. Typewriters are individual — more so than handwriting sometimes. That machine is lying about somewhere and not too far away either, I imagine.'

'Right, sir.' Whittaker picked the papers up in the clip and left the office. Garth sat back in his swivel chair and chewed at his cheroot pensively.

'Derek Collins or Dudley Morton,' he murmured, glancing at his watch. 'Hmmm — I can get at our smug stockbroker friend any time but I can't pick and choose with young Derek. Better go there.'

When Whittaker came back into the office he motioned to him. 'We're going to see our twelve-year-old friend, Whitty. Get him in the lunch hour. Bring your notebook.'

The Sergeant nodded and followed Garth downstairs to the car. During the journey Garth sat lost in thought. Now and again he grinned tightly to himself.

'Y'know, Whitty, it's the simple things in life that get us by the nose sometimes! Those five matchboxes, for instance. It's really so simple that I could wince.'

'Yes, sir,' Whittaker said moodily. He couldn't ask questions because, being a good driver, he wanted to keep his attention on the road.

13

When they arrived at 18, Calver Terrace the poker-faced Milly opened the door and admitted them into the drawing room as on their previous visit. Mrs. Collins came hurrying in, and something of the coldness when she had been at Scotland Yard the previous evening still seemed to be lingering about her.

'How are you, gentlemen? What's the trouble this time?'

Garth rose beside Whittaker and glanced at his watch. 'I had hoped, madam, that your son might be here.'

'He's having his dinner.' Beatrice Collins looked at Garth entreatingly. 'Mr. Garth, why do you have to keep pestering the boy? You know as well as I do that at his age he hasn't anything to do with this terrible business.'

Garth's iron-hard expression relaxed slightly. 'I'm not here to upset the boy, Mrs. Collins, but I have reason to believe that he holds the key to one of the biggest problems in this whole business. I'm sure you will want him to speak just as much as I do — if only to bring your husband's killer to justice.'

The woman's lips tightened a little; then she turned to the doorway and called into the hall. 'Derek, come here a minute! Quickly!'

Somewhere a door banged and a second or two later the boy came hurrying in. He slowed down to a stop and looked at Garth sheepishly as he met the pale eyes.

'Remember me, son?' Garth grinned and sat down in the armchair so he could be more on the boy's level. 'Come here a minute and tell me something . . . '

Derek hesitated, glanced at his mother's set face, then he walked to where Garth was seated.

'I'm not really the big, tough guy you seem to think, you know,' Garth smiled. 'Got a boy of my own a bit older than yourself, and I know the things they get up to — like you with your matchboxes, for instance.'

Small lips set tightly. The round chin quivered a little.

'Don't you think you'd get on better, son, if you told me the truth? That those five matchboxes each contained one living butterfly?'

Whittaker looked blank. Mrs. Collins gave a start and stared at her son fixedly.

'It's all perfectly simple.' Garth's genial smile showed he was enjoying his little sensation. 'Our research department advised me that the matchboxes contained traces of phosphorus, wood slivers, minute quantities of scale-like material, pollen, and tobacco dust.' He spread his hands. 'Possibly these ingredients might have been picked up in your husband's travels, madam — out of the very dust of the air itself. But, to me, pollen and scale-like material suggested something else. The wings of a butterfly are made of minute scales, giving them their colouring, and the allusion to pollen dust when thinking of butterflies is obvious. I remembered what I often did in my youth during the summer months, and the matchboxes being drilled with air holes confirmed the simple solution.'

Suddenly Garth's smile was gone as his cold eyes aimed questions at Derek.

'Yes, sir, I did have butterflies in those boxes,' he admitted, hanging his head. 'I intended pinning them on a card.'

'Derek!' His mother's voice was horrified. 'Of all the fiendish ideas — '

' 'Tisn't!' he objected, looking at her. 'Lots of boys in my class do it. You should see John Hardwick's collection! He's got a whacking big — '

'Never mind John Hardwick for the moment,' Garth said. 'You were told by your father that putting those butterflies in matchboxes was a terrible crime, weren't you?'

Derek gave a start, his brown eyes wide.

'Yes — he told me that, mister, and he also said something about crimes always being reported to the police. That was why I kept quiet — I was afraid, because you are the police, aren't you?'

'Along with some other chaps,' Garth acknowledged. 'So thinking you had committed a crime you kept quiet, and you had also to keep quiet because of it being found out that you played truant from school yesterday morning eh?'

'Oh Lor'!' Derek said in dismay.

'Is this true?' his mother asked sharply. 'Derek, did you play truant yesterday morning?'

'Yes — ' Derek looked from one to the other wildly. 'I didn't really mean to, only — well, when I got near the school it was half an hour past time and it was such a lovely morning. Besides, Mr. Gunther is such a pig when you're late . . .'

'Well, lad, while not upholding truants in the slightest degree I must say that you wouldn't be a genuine schoolboy without at least one to your credit,' Garth remarked. 'I did it myself now and again, you know — ' His face became stern again, 'What about the afternoon? How did you get by without a note of explanation?'

'That's just it,' Derek muttered. 'Old Gunther is still waiting for it. I've been scared stiff.'

'Well I don't know!' Beatrice Collins exclaimed. 'And how did you know, Mr. Garth?'

'Oh, I get about,' he answered, shrugging. 'But now that is disposed of, let me tell *you* something, Derek, and you can see if I'm right, eh? Yesterday morning your father came in your bedroom and woke you up to warn you about being late. Then, wanting a light for his cigarette, he looked round and happened to see five matchboxes on the dressing table. He opened one, saw a butterfly, and shut it again. He flew into a rage, warned you what would happen if you committed such a crime again, and then stuffed the boxes in his pocket.'

Derek gave a little gulp. 'You — you weren't there, mister, were you?'

'No, but I have ways of finding things out. Am I right?'

'Yes, sir. He asked if there were butterflies in the other boxes. And when he told me never to say anything or do it again I didn't, since it was such a crime. I didn't know it was, honest. Lots of my pals do it. But I thought I'd better keep things to myself.'

'Just let butterflies stay where they are in future, son; you will know why as you get older. You're too nice a lad to be cruel. Well, madam — ' he beamed on Mrs. Collins and squared his shoulders — 'I think that clears things up here.'

'I still want to know how you learned exactly what happened,' she said levelly.

Garth hesitated and then motioned to the boy. The woman understood and nodded.

'Go and finish your dinner, Derek,' she said briefly. 'And don't worry any more. I'll see you get a note to take back to Mr. Gunther.' She shook her head helplessly as the boy clattered out into the hall. 'Well, Inspector?'

'Your husband, madam, suffered from extreme claustrophobia — which is one word explaining all his strange eccentricities of character. I see no harm in you knowing the fact since you suffered a good deal from the effects of those foibles.'

'Of course,' she said slowly. 'Fear of confined spaces. I've heard of that. That would explain it, wouldn't it?'

'It does. To a man of claustrophobic tendencies the thought of butterflies shut in a box would represent the acme of crime, but to a — forgive me — bloodthirsty schoolboy it would be a mere trifle. I remembered you saying that your husband had an unlighted cigarette. Since his vantage point when you found him was the dressing table, he had probably seen the matchboxes there and opened one to look for a match. He saw a butterfly, asked about the other boxes — as Derek has proved — and stuffed the boxes in his pockets. Afterwards, his preoccupation in arguing with you caused him to forget them. That is my assumption. Since he is dead we can never prove it.'

Beatrice Collins gave a faint smile. 'Well, Inspector, I'm glad to know that you have finished worrying my boy. It is something a mother always resents.'

'I know, and you have been more than cooperative. There is just one more thing. Did you ever hear your husband speak of a Mr. Dudley Morton, or his wife?'

'Morton? No, Mr. Garth. I never heard the name.'

'I see,' Garth said. 'All right then,

thanks. I'll keep in touch with you. Ready, Whitty?'

With a nod Whittaker followed him out into the hall and Beatrice Collins saw them down the pathway. Back in the car again Garth took out a cheroot and lit up.

'See what I mean by 'simple'?' he asked, grinning.

'Yes, sir — and I could kick myself. Just a side issue, eh?'

'Side issue be damned! It may just be that it's still the key to the whole darned business. Look at it this way — imprisoning butterflies constituted a ghastly crime to Collins. How much more of a crime would it seem to him if somebody human were imprisoned, or murdered, in a cupboard or something . . . '

Garth's eyes became blank for a moment. He took his cheroot from his mouth unconsciously.

'That ear,' he breathed. 'Cupboard . . . claustrophobia . . . Suffering snakes, I feel something slipping into place! And he was just as claustrophobic fifteen years ago as he was yesterday morning. Mmmm . . . ' he grinned widely. 'Take no

183

notice of me, Whitty — just the memory putting in a spot of overtime.'

'Yes, sir,' Whittaker muttered, with a dubious glance. 'Getting back to this butterfly business — ' he swung the wheel fiercely as a cyclist wobbled precariously in front of the bonnet — 'after Collins went out of the house with the boxes in his pockets, what happened then?'

'Oh, that? He got to his office before he remembered them, perhaps when he felt in his pockets for his keys. He opened the boxes with a certain ceremony — like opening prison doors — and that left the five matchboxes in a row on his desk. Then he opened the window to let the butterflies go outside. Remember that I questioned if he had opened it purely for fresh air? No reason why I should tell all this to Mrs. Collins.'

'And then . . . Collins died,' Whittaker said grimly. 'Shot through the heart.'

'That,' Garth said, inhaling deeply, 'is not so simple. But there are one or two theories to fit it which I'll try later.'

They did not return to the office immediately but stopped at the *Welcome*

Café for lunch. It was towards half past two when Garth was settling again at his desk, the wry look of dyspepsia on his face and in his pale eyes. For several minutes he sat studying his notes, then he got to his feet again.

'I'm going on a prowl,' he said briefly. 'That ear of Morton's worries me. While I'm gone do what you can over the 'phone to check the various alibis. If you want me I'll either be in 'Crow' or the Calligraphy Department.'

'Okay, sir.'

Garth wandered down the long corridor outside his office and finished up in the broad, sunny reaches of the Calligraphy Department. He nodded to the various workers who glanced at him and finally singled out Albert Knott, chief of the department. A gnome-like man in an overall, he was poring over a sheet of glass ruled into squares, overlying the original warning note sent to the Assistant Commissioner. Above the glass sheet was an enlarging camera with the lens ready for action.

'Well, does it sit up and beg?' Garth

asked him, watching.

'It will before I'm finished with it.' Knott looked up briefly and reached out his hand to pass a photo-enlargement. 'Here is a specimen of the warning, magnified. Take a look.'

Garth considered the huge letters, every deficiency revealed, every little blur and point magnified to pin-sharp detail. Knott got the glass slide to his liking and relaxed for a moment.

'Fortunately,' he said, 'typewriter manufacturers all have a more or less distinctive style of type-fount. The expert can pick 'em out anywhere. Even the letters themselves change regularly — a little ear off the 'g' — a tiny peak off the central serif of the 'w' and so on. All of which brings this note back to having been typed on a Model Seven, Valiant Noiseless Typewriter. It's not a well-known make, which is a help. Application to the manufacturers should furnish you with a complete list of the retailers and that should narrow your field. It's a British make by the way. Birmingham firm I think.'

Garth rubbed his hands. 'This is the

kind of action I like! And those specimens I dug up? Any of them tally?'

'No. Nothing to do with it. And the paper — well, on the original warning it is 'Dampdew Parchment', manufactured, according to my list, by the Essex Paper Company. All you can do is use the same process of elimination by applying to the manufacturers and from them getting on to the retailers. There's a fingerprint report with the note,' Knott added. 'Nothing to do with me. I was sending it in to you. Here, read it.'

Garth took it and wrinkled his nose.

'Barren as a desert except for smudges — probably my own or the Assistant Commissioner's . . . and mashing where erasures or prints have been made. Well, I expected it.'

'There is another point in regard to this typing,' Knott added, considering it under the glass slide. 'It was executed by an expert. The expert, you see, has an easy rhythm of movement, which makes for a more or less continuous smooth alignment of characters. The machine too, was apparently brand new. The amateur, due to nick and hit methods, strikes some letters harder than others, and sometimes too quickly, resulting in many of the letters being slightly misplaced. The fact that an expert did the job may help you, but there isn't much else. I've one or two enlargements to make and then I'll file them away in readiness for comparison with the Valiant machines you happen to locate.'

'I could kiss you,' Garth murmured, pushing the fingerprint report in his pocket. 'As soon as I get something substantial I'll be pestering you again.'

Returning to his own office he found Whittaker at the telephone, solemn-faced and listening. He said 'Thanks!' briefly to somebody at the other end of the line and then returned the instrument to its cradle.

'Evelyn Drew didn't get to her office until ten yesterday morning, sir,' he said quietly, making a note. 'That was her firm I was speaking to.'

'Didn't she, though?' Garth reflected. 'Try the others while you're at it, Whitty. When you've finished that, look up the telephone number of the Valiant Type-writer Company — somewhere in Birmingham, I think — and try and find out to which retailers they have sold machines. Cover back a few years and let me have a list. Do the same for the Essex Paper Company and find out which retailers have bought Dampdew Parchment. I'm carrying on to try and get that ear problem out of my system.'

Whittaker blew out his cheeks expressively and nodded. With a grin Garth went out again. In a few minutes he was in the Crime Index Department — usually known as M.O. in short for *Modus Operandi* — of the Criminal Records Office. His cheroot extinguished and a look of anguished concentration on his face he went across the airy, well-lighted room with its array of oak index cabinets to Superintendent Richard Billings, the man with the encyclopedic mind in charge of this particular section of files and records.

'Offhand, Dick, I don't know exactly what I'm looking for, but I've got to find it!' Garth threw himself on Superintendent Billings' mercy. 'Call me a dam' fool and kick me out if you like. But it's something about a man's ear that I want to check up. I believe it goes back fifteen years. And I seem to remember, vaguely, that it was a murder case.'

'You don't help a fellow much, do you? Murder case fifteen years ago, eh? Hmmm — ' Billings pondered. 'Well, I'll dump the stuff in your lap and you can do the rest. Wait here a moment.'

Garth nodded and sat down at a reading desk. After a while Billings returned with an assortment of ledger-like dossiers Garth groaned at the number of them, hunched himself forward and began to sort them out. He had reached the sixth, marked 'Uncompleted' in red ink before he suddenly found something.

'Got it! This is it!'

Billings looked and nodded off-handedly. 'Vincent Darricourt, eh? Convicted for embezzlement and got five years, and then five years later he got himself mixed up in a murder business that never came to trial. You'll find the case incomplete.'

'Yes, I remember it now.' Garth was gazing intently at a variety of photographs, particularly the right profile, all of the same person. His memory was working fast, going back to a day fifteen years before, when he had studied these self-same photographs and noted the peculiar right ear. His gaze shifted to the fingerprint impressions and then to the brief notation underneath —

Vincent. Darricourt. Age 30. Sentenced to 5 years penal servitude for . . .

There was a good deal more which did not particularly interest Garth. It was the man's face! Thick dark hair parted in the centre, a close-cropped black moustache adorning the long upper lip — that long upper lip! — which was slightly drawn away to reveal irregular teeth.

'Yes, I remember him now,' Garth repeated. 'In those days I was Detective-Sergeant Garth, fancy free and without indigestion. Mmm . . . Good old Chief Inspector Dawlish! He handled it — *of course!*'

He looked up sharply as Billings stood watching idly.

'That's the ear,' Garth said grimly. 'Several of the boys, including myself, were shown the photographic profiles. I remember the ear, and still do. We studied the photographs in case the chap couldn't be located. I picked him up finally at a cottage in Sussex and Bannister picked up the wife and maid somewhere. That was as far as I got. The Chief never went out of his way to tell me anything . . .'

Garth's eyes dropped to the reports, unclassified, just as they had been gathered at the time of the case, and he read carefully. The first report was dated August 10th, fifteen years ago.

Report of Divisional-Inspector Bronson Called this morning at 8-57 a.m. to the home of Vincent Darricourt, Stockbroker, of 49 Calvin Lane, Hampstead, and found the body of a woman about 55 suspended by the neck from the roof beam of a hall clothes cupboard. Took the usual statement and had housekeeper sign it (separate). House-keeper — Mrs. Emily Grayson — denied all knowledge of the affair and stated that her employers, Mr. and Mrs. Dar-ricourt, together with the maid Bella, were away on holiday. Finding no traces as to how the crime had been commit-ted I contacted Scotland Yard and . . .

Garth sniffed and turned to the observations of his predecessor Chief Inspector Dawlish.

'Clothes Cupboard Mystery'.
Confidential Conclusions of C.I. Herbert Dawlish: I am struck by the fact that Vincent Darricourt and his wife Ruby chose this time for a holiday at their cottage. Have given instruc-tions for both — with maid — to be picked up. Have traced Vincent Darri-court from C.R.O., and he is recorded as a convicted embezzler who was released only recently. Have ordered my men to commit his photograph to memory in case he should try to 'skip'. No photograph of Ruby Darricourt

seems to be available at the Darricourt's home — and since she has never been convicted of a criminal offence we have of course no records concerning her. I have her description, however — smallish, dark-haired, blue-eyed. See separate report . . .

Ruby Darricourt: Height about 5ft. 4ins., hair brown, eyes blue, slim build. Aged about 27.

The murdered woman has been identified as Mrs. Beryl Cleveland, a wealthy recluse, and apparently something of an eccentric. Lived by herself in a small villa on the South Downs five miles out of Worthing. She never seemed to have visitors and there are no neighbours near enough to give evidence as to her movements. Investigation through the documents in her home reveal the interesting fact that certain speculations she had made recently through Darricourt's firm would have netted her yet another fortune — at Darricourt's expense — had she lived. That is all I know. I can think that he hanged her to stop her speculations materializing — and since they were personal they could not pass to anybody else at her death — but I can't prove it. I know too that Darricourt does not run his own business on the square, but again I cannot show beyond a shadow of doubt that this is a fact.

It is about one of the most clueless crimes I ever came across. No traces whatever. I am hoping I shall find Darricourt, his wife Ruby, or both . . .

Garth nodded to himself, lighted a fresh cheroot, and turned the dossier's leaves slowly. He paused again after a moment.

(Report by Divisional-Inspector Sampson)
Identification: Beryl Cleveland. Aged 56. Height 5ft. 7 ins. Very heavy build. Grey eyes and hair. Complexion normally sallow. Recluse. Lived 25 years in 'Downshouse,' an isolated villa on the Downs 5 miles from Worthing. Post Mortem Report: Beryl Cleveland

(decd.). *Death caused by strangulation from hanging. When body was found it had been dead approximately nine hours.*

Note by Chief Inspector Dawlish: Found at 9 a.m. Murder occurred at approximately midnight. Suicide unlikely. Am convinced housekeeper is blameless. She would never have strength to lift a woman of Beryl Cleveland's weight.

Turning the dossier pages, Garth came to one that made him grin reminiscently . . .

*August 11*th.

Vincent Darricourt was picked up today by Detective-Sergeant Garth at Darricourt's Sussex cottage. When questioned, Darricourt stated that his wife was out walking and that the maid, who is also a companion-help, had gone with her. Detective-Sergeant Bannister stayed to await their return and apprehended them later in the day.

In statement, details attached, Darricourt stated that he and his wife had decided to stay at the cottage for a week or two, and it having no radio or television, and there being no newspapers delivered, he was not aware of what had happened. As far as can be told — and I have nothing to prove to the contrary — this statement is correct . . . Fingerprints of Vincent Darricourt check with those taken at the time of his conviction for embezzlement.

Darricourt admitted that Miss Cleveland was a client of his but denied all responsibility for the crime. I also questioned one Granville Collins today. He is head clerk to Darricourt. His movements seem to have been a little irregular during the night of the murder. He went out in his car, it broke down, and he says he came home about 3 a.m.

Apparently he went to see Darricourt over a business matter, failed to find him at home and then spent part of the night putting his car right. I personally do not believe him but since I cannot prove otherwise my personal conclusions cannot be submitted in evidence.

I cannot see that he (Collins) would gain anything by murdering Beryl Cleveland . . .

Garth smiled tightly and turned still further into the pages, paused yet again —

Continuation of conclusions by Dawlish: In her statement, Mrs. Darricourt denied that she went with her husband to Sussex. She states she went ahead separately by train, the maid travelling with her husband in the car.

To me several factors are obvious. The Darricourts, and maid, left for the country the evening before the deceased was found hanging in the clothes cupboard . . . The Darricourts could somehow have hanged her before leaving and left it to the housekeeper to finally come upon her; they could have strangled her outside and brought the body back to the house — strangling her in such a way that the cord mark would be in the same place when she was hanged in the cupboard. But again I have no proof, not even anything incriminating enough for spectrograph analysis. Nobody seems to have seen the Darricourts' car on the way to the cottage, but it is checked with the ticket inspector that Ruby Darricourt went by train.

On the dead woman's clothing there are traces of dust, burrs, and slight grass stains which considering her country home is not unexpected. Probably from her garden.

Charges cannot be preferred until new evidence is forthcoming. Vincent Darricourt and his wife were released today from custody. The maid, after her preliminary statement, which corroborated that of her employers, was allowed to leave . . .

'Inspector,' Garth murmured, closing the dossier slowly, 'don't turn in your grave, but I think you missed something! You don't object if the flat-footed one-time Detective-Sergeant Garth reopens the darned thing, do you?'

He got to his feet, nodded his thanks to Billings as he put the dossier down, then went out of the room

14

When Garth got back to his office he found Whittaker just at the close of typing out some notes at his own desk.

'As you know, sir, Evelyn Drew has no alibi,' he said, glancing up. 'That chap Howard Farrow is okay. He *is* employed in the surveyor's office and he *was* surveying in the Terancy Street region yesterday morning. I also telephoned that girl Mary Baxter's home, and she did oversleep.'

'Just make a note of it,' Garth said, with a touch of impatience. 'I've other things on my mind concerning an incomplete dossier about Vincent Darricourt. Dudley Morton, and Darricourt, a man who served sentence for embezzlement and then got mixed up in a murder case, only to be freed because of insufficient evidence against him, are one and the same man. I traced that ear angle. His wife Ruby was in on it too, apparently, but the charge couldn't be made to stick any more than that against her husband.'

Whittaker waited expectantly for further revelations.

'The case in which he was involved was the 'Clothes Cupboard Mystery', as the newspapers poetically put it . . . ' Garth went to his swivel chair and dropped into it. 'Which fact starts to make a lot of things tie up. A wealthy recluse by the name of Beryl Cleveland was found dead in a clothes cupboard in the hall of the Darricourt house and the evidence showed that she had been hanged — in the cupboard. But it couldn't be proved exactly what had happened, hence the dropping of the charge. A maid named Bella was in on it too. Now, Whitty, do you feel something knock?'

'Claustrophobia, you mean?'

'Possibly, yes. Anyway, the business smacks of it.' Garth lighted a cheroot. 'Claustrophobia. We've already seen how our woolly-minded friend Granville Collins was affected because of imprisoned butterflies — how much more would he have gone off the deep end had he seen, or otherwise known, of a woman hanging dead in a clothes cupboard? Remember I mentioned a connection this morning?

'To be honest, though, I hadn't then consciously linked the business with the fifteen-year-old 'Clothes Cupboard Mystery', even though I had a hand in it. Maybe my subconscious was working Ear — Morton — fifteen-year-old case — and hazily, a clothes cupboard with its definitely claustral atmosphere . . . Mmmm — Fifteen years ago Granville Collins was employed by Vincent Darricourt. Fifteen years ago Darricourt — Morton — decided to pay Granville Collins two-fifty pounds a week. Fifteen years ago Collins was a small-fry stockbroker, just started in business on his own, when Evelyn Drew started with him. All right, it's easier to believe that Morton paid Collins that money to make him keep his mouth shut than to retain him as a wizard of stock-broking prescience.'

'Right you are, sir.' It was Whittaker's turn to brood. 'This may start proving the motive, sir,' he said at last. 'We can assume that somehow Collins saw Morton — or Darricourt as he was then — murder this woman in a clothes cupboard; we can also assume that for reasons best known to himself Collins decided to try blackmail instead of revealing his knowledge to the police and getting Darricourt all tied up with the law — but we can't *prove* it! Any more than it could be proved then.'

Garth grinned. 'Pass me that statement of Evelyn Drew's, will you?'

Whittaker searched through the papers and handed over the statement he had typed. Garth read it through carefully, then nodded.

'I thought she said that 'he had just started in business for himself,' That is, fifteen years ago. That, my bonny boy, is significant!'

'It is?'

'It is significant because prior to that he must have been employed by Darricourt. Since Collins was Darricourt's head clerk he certainly picked up his stockbroking knowledge from that source, and was also perhaps in a position to know the facts behind, or about, the 'Clothes Cupboard' murder.'

'That's a logical possibility, sir, yes,' Whittaker agreed slowly, 'but of course we have to prove it.'

'Of course we have!' Garth exploded. 'It's simply that I'm struggling to find a solid piece in this slippery business.' He heaved out an arm towards the telephone. 'All right, so Collins was employed by Darricourt. Let's get it as indisputable fact, eh? We can also see when Collins started in business for himself. By law, just as applicable fifteen years ago as it is today, an employer must keep his employee's insurance book stamped up. And also by law an employee must surrender his book when he starts in business for himself, getting a dated receipt for it. Even though Darricourt changed his name — probably because of the social scandal over the body in the cupboard — I don't see that Collins would have to — '

A minute later Garth was through to the appropriate Government department.

'Inspector Garth here, C.I.D. Turn up

your files for fifteen years ago, will you please, and see if you can trace an employer by the name of Vincent Darricourt, business address unknown, but he was a stockbroker if that's any guide. He should have had an employee by the name of Granville Collins — eh? Yes, it would certainly be in the city area, perhaps even Throgmorton Street. Right. Yes, call me back.'

Sighing, Garth sat back and waited. Within a very short time the telephone rang sharply.

He picked the instrument up. 'Yes, Inspector Garth speaking — Eh? Oh, the post office!' His eyes hardened and for a moment he drew more hurriedly at his cheroot. 'Yes . . . I see. Right!'

He put the 'phone down again and slapped his hands on the desk.

'Now that *is* interesting! There were no mails delivered to the home of Dudley Morton yesterday morning!'

'But he said — '

'Evidently he was lying,' Garth snapped. 'As I suspected — but that doesn't alter the unpleasant fact that he talked to his wife on the 'phone while the murder took place. Pity.'

'Y'know,' Whittaker said wistfully, 'I could take a lot more interest in these side issues, if I could only fathom how Collins died in his office with nobody near him.'

Garth gave a cynical grin. 'I've got a theory about that, but theories can knock you out cold when you get into court, or even as far as an arrest. Until I prove my theory I'm busy on the other details and leaving that major riddle until last. I — '

Again the telephone rang. He listened absently, threw his cheroot in the tray and then said, 'Thanks very much.

'One load less to carry anyway,' he commented, hanging up. 'Vincent Darricourt did employ Granville Collins fifteen years ago as a head clerk, at nineteen Cathcart Street. Collins surrendered his book on November twelfth, three months after the clothes cupboard business. Now I wonder,' he mused, 'if you could get your teeth pulled out and new ones imbedded into your gums in that time? Yes, I imagine you could if you were normally healthy.'

Whittaker looked blank, then frowned as a new thought seized him.

'Do you suppose, sir, that Darricourt changed his name to Morton legally?'

'Offhand I'd say no. When you come mighty close to being accused of murder, and when somebody knows what you did and is blackmailing you on that account it isn't politic to change your name by Deed Poll and let everybody know about it. It might arouse suspicion on the part of the law as to why. No, I think it was done illegally, perhaps to try and sidetrack Collins, which obviously did not work. Just as I might make a fatal mistake on a case and thereafter creep about under the monicker of Jack Robinson or something.'

Whittaker began to shuffle the notes and inspect them carefully. Garth knew the signs. Something was bothering him.

'Haven't we gone round a prop and achieved precisely nothing? We haven't proved that Darricourt is Morton; we're even further from proving that Darricourt — alias Morton — killed Collins. We haven't proved that Morton's telephone conversation alibi is false; we haven't proved that Collins was blackmailing Morton. It's all pure assumption even though all the facts seem to be there. And we don't know that Collins ever did see the clothes cupboard murder.'

'And we don't know that the sun is losing thousands of tons of mass a minute, but in the absence of anything else we — or at any rate the physicists — are entitled to assume it,' Garth answered heavily. 'Suffering snakes, man, of course it's assumption! First you assume from given premises, then you infer every conceivable possibility from the premises, and finally you prove.'

'Yes, sir.' Whittaker looked chastened. 'I'd better get through to the Valiant Typewriter Company, hadn't I? I've got their address and was going to 'phone them when you came in.'

Garth was scribbling busily and he nodded. 'Yes, get on with it. I'm jotting down the points in order of 'Proof Required'.' He glared. 'That ought to satisfy you. While you're busy on that 'phone I'm going to the Radio Department.'

He got to his feet and left the office, arriving presently in the laboratory where the tall, bald-headed Dr. Pierce held sway. He grinned mischievously as he saw the Chief Inspector striding ponderously amidst the electric and scientific equipment.

'Hello there, Mort! Come for a look round?'

Garth studied him coldly. 'I want a look at that sound-tape of the Dictaphone voices. All the trimmings.'

'Sure thing. Step into the projection theatre and I'll be with you.'

Garth went inside amidst the gloom of amber lighting. He settled down, staring at the dim grey rectangle of screen at the end of the long room. Presently Pierce's white-overalled figure came in and joined him. He picked up a telephone at his elbow.

'Okay, Tommy, let's have it,' he said.

The amber ceiling lights expired. A beam flashed from above and on the screen there appeared along its top half something resembling the saw teeth of a mountain range, etched dead black against white background.

'There we have the magnified sound track of a man's voice — Dudley Morton's,' Pierce said, the top of his bald head gleaming from the reflection of the steady ray above him. 'Sound on film recording is simply the transformation of electrical vibrations — sounds to you — by electronic processes into *visible* sound impulses, the result appearing like the teeth of a saw, or in the old fashioned way like Jacob's Ladder, the rungs of same having infinite variations of thickness according to the impulse received. Then, by photo-electric processes — '

'Just a minute, man, hold your horses! What I want to know is could anybody ever imitate anybody else's voice — on a sound track, I mean, and get away with it?'

'Like hell they could,' Pierce replied calmly. 'Voices, let me tell you, are a new damning factor in the eternal parade of science versus crime. Nature, thank God, never creates the same thing twice over.

Voices are in the same category as fingerprints. They can never be disguised. To the ear, yes — but to the sound track, never! Certain inflections always remain ineradicable.'

'Even though there might be slight distortion, like over a 'phone and Dictaphone, as in this case?'

'Even so — but 'phones and Dictaphones are accurate reproducers in these days, remember.' Pierce waved towards the screen. 'You might call this a spectrograph projection of the voice, only instead of being spectrum analysis of some bit of metal or dust, it is analysis of sound. That saw-tooth you are looking at is Dudley Morton's voice saying one of the most common words in the language — 'the'.'

Garth stared at the screen through narrowed eyes. 'All that mass of mountains for the one word 'the'?'

'Don't forget that the magnification is enormous. Run through an ordinary sound gate and exciter equipment it would be gone in a flash. Every peak and valley, as we call 'em, is there, Garth. That is the word 'the', chosen because we utter it more, as a rule, than any other word. Now let me show you something else.'

Pierce lifted the telephone again.

'Let's have the other one, Tommy,' he said; and there appeared on the lower half of the screen another mountain range — at first apparently the same, until Pierce got up and went to the screen, pulled a switch and a transparent network of graph-like wires, stretched on a frame and mathematically perfect, exactly covered the screen.

'This is what we check 'em with,' Pierce explained. 'This second lot we've got on the lower half is Morton's wife saying the same word 'the'. Notice the difference in valleys and peaks? Not one is the same as the ones above.'

Garth leaned his arms on the back of the chair in front of him, fascinated. Pierce came back to the telephone again.

'Tommy, let's have that second one of the 'the' from Morton.'

The telephone went back on its rest and the lower half image of Mrs. Morton's 'the' blanked out of sight.

Another one came in view and slid to a stop. Line for line, square for square, fraction for fraction, it exactly matched the majority of the peaks and valleys in the track above.

'See what I mean?' Pierce asked. 'That is the same man saying the same word. There are discrepancies, of course, caused by respiratory irregularity perhaps, or by a slight congestion of the vocal cords. We work on a 'majority-tally'. That is, in words spoken by the same voice certain peaks and valleys must correspond, as points correspond in fingerprints. In the case of the voice of another person no points correspond with anybody's but that person.'

Pierce pressed a button and the table and the images vanished. The orange lights came up again in the ceiling. Garth sat back in his chair.

'Black magic — that's what you backroom boys dabble in!' he commented. 'Anyway, thanks for the demonstration ... only I didn't come entirely for that. I want my office wired for recording — a mike, I mean, with recording apparatus and all the trappings in an adjoining office. I also want a bell fixed too which, when I press it, means that I want you boys to start recording.'

'Okay, we'll go to work on it right away.'

Garth nodded and got to his feet. 'I'll let you know whose voice is whose when the time comes — and thanks.'

He left the projection theatre, returned through the laboratory and back to his own office. When he entered he found Jessop and Finnigan, both of them looking very moody, waiting. Whittaker, for his part, seemed to be controlling some inner excitement.

'Well?' Garth asked the two plain-clothes men briefly.

'Nothing, sir,' Jessop answered, acting as spokesman. 'We've turned Amberly Building inside out — punched it, pounded it, and done everything except blast it, and we even did that, metaphorically. It doesn't yield a sausage.'

'Hmmm . . . Well, there it is. And you

left whatshisname — that constable — on duty?'

'Yes, sir, awaiting your orders.'

Garth nodded and jerked his head towards the door. The two PC men went out and the Chief Inspector reached for the telephone. Within a matter of moments he had made arrangements for the guardian constable to be relieved, and given instructions for Amberly Building to be kept under continuous observation. Then he turned to eye Whittaker.

'What have you got, Whitty?'

'I have here fourteen firms in the city who have Valiant typewriters in stock, and here are the addresses. Plenty of choice . . . unfortunately.'

Garth took the list and ran his eyes down it. 'A sample will have to be obtained from each machine, and the serial number of that particular machine and the shop stocking it noted down,' he said. 'If any of 'em have been loaned out, find out to whom, when, and all about it. I'm putting you on that job, Whitty my boy — and get Calthorpe and Mason to help you.'

'Right, sir — and here's a list of retailers for the Dampdew Parchment. In the city there are thirty stationers all stocking it.'

'Okay — hop to that too, and if I don't see you for years I'll quite understand. Get invoice copies of every firm to whom this paper has been sold, as far back as you can reasonably go. You don't have to soft-pedal anything. Let them know where you're from so you can get all the necessary facts. As for me — I'm off to Kensington to take a look at a person so far not in our little picture. Mrs. Morton, to be exact. I want to discover whom this woman is who is so devoted to her husband's business that she'll take up fifteen minutes reading him a letter that the postman never delivered . . . And besides,' Garth looked about him, 'this office is going to be invaded by the sound-recording fiends. I'm having it wired.'

Whittaker did not ask why. He was feeling rather appalled by the amount of searching he had ahead of him. With a grin Garth reached for his hat.

'Carry on until six, Whitty, then come back here and let's see how far you've got. We'll have a check over and then get home. I've got to finish my competition crossword this week or I'll never get it in the post in time.'

He turned and left the office, fragrant cheroot haze drifting behind him.

15

It was half past four when Garth, driving himself in an official car, pulled up outside a massive Georgian-style residence in the Kensington district. It was an impersonal place, detached from the similar style houses around it and having a small portico with the usual rounded pillars supporting it. The front garden, though brief as becomes so many London houses, was faultlessly kept.

Seizing the griffin-knocker, Garth thumped it hard on the green door and presently a middle-aged maid appeared.

'Good afternoon . . . ' Garth smiled genially. 'I wonder if I might have a few words with Mrs. Morton? Garth is the name — Inspector Garth, Scotland Yard.'

'If you will step inside, sir?'

'Thank you.' Garth moved into the well-kept hall with its array of brass antiques, plaques, and armoury. There was a backdrop of dark oak panels and a staircase receding into gloomy upper regions.

Then the maid reappeared from one of the doors leading off the hall. 'If you will step this way, Inspector?'

Garth studied the maid unobtrusively. She was trimly dressed in a black uniform and white cap — but all the care of her attire could not disguise the overflowing flesh of years. She was certainly nearer fifty than forty, well built, and impassive looking. Her voice and manner, for her station, seemed unusually educated —

Then Garth was past her and into a large room with two enormous windows admitting the streaming afternoon sunlight. It singled out costly antique furniture here and there, but in the main the appointments were modern. Standing beside one of the further windows so that the sunshine caught the silver glints in her otherwise dark hair was a smallish, slender woman. As he entered she turned quickly to him.

'*Good* afternoon, Inspector Garth. Please have a seat, won't you?'

'Thank you, madam.' Garth took care

to seat himself with his back to the light so he could study the woman more closely.

She was not as old as he had somehow expected. Records had said she had been twenty-seven fifteen years ago. Must now be forty-two . . . Mmmm — Five feet four, slim. About that height, yes, but she had, now he came to notice, more plumpness than he had at first imagined. Grey streaks in the brown hair.

Her eyes were blue, as the record had said, her features interesting without being good looking. Most unexpected was her infectious, friendly smile.

'You won't believe this, Inspector,' she said, settling on the divan opposite him, 'but I was seriously contemplating either ringing you up or coming over to Scotland Yard to see you. I'm so glad you called . . . You would like some tea, I'm sure?'

She pressed the bell push. The stolid middle-aged maid appeared.

'Yes, m'm?'

'Oh, Bella — tea please, and do see that it is nice and hot . . . '

Garth was finding it confoundedly hard to dislike the woman. As a younger woman she must have been definitely adorable — the bubbly-cuddly kind.

'Er — madam, I didn't really come here on a social call, you know. I'm afraid it is most official. You say you were coming over to the Yard. Might I ask why?'

She spread dainty hands. 'I was simply coming over to tell you that my husband was speaking the truth — about the letter I telephoned to him, mean. He rang me up during this morning and told me of his interview with you. We're so close to each other, Dudley and I, you know.' A far-away look came in her very blue eyes. 'Poor dear, he seemed so upset. Naturally I told him there was nothing to worry about. I said I would soon convince you ... Since you've come of your own accord, though, that saves me a lot of trouble, doesn't it?'

'It would appear so, madam, yes.' Garth had the oddest feeling of embarrassment, as though he were walking into a quiet church in squeaky shoes.

221

'Ah, Bella! Splendid!' Mrs. Morton waved a hand vaguely as the maid came in pushing a tea-wagon. 'Bella, put it there. I'll attend to it.'

'Yes, m'm.'

Garth sat back, morosely watching the woman's hands flitting like dragonflies over the glitter of silver tea ware and polished crockery.

'Sugar, Mr. Garth?'

'One, thank you,' he growled, and silently thanked heaven that Sergeant Whittaker had not come with him.

'You'll have a cake, Mr. Garth?'

He took a bun from a silver cake dish and cleared his throat.

'I don't usually indulge myself between meals — dyspeptic, you know.'

'Oh, really? The curse of civilization I believe it's called — or is it cancer?' She shrugged. 'I'm so terribly vague about such things. Dear Dudley does all the thinking for me . . . '

'Madam, I do not wish to seem rude, but — how long were you telephoning your husband yesterday morning when you read him the business letter?'

'Oh, a dreadful time!'

Garth drank some of the tea and took a bite out of his cake. He marvelled silently at the brilliant way the woman managed to remain entirely feminine even though tackling a singularly squashy cream éclair.

'As long as fifteen minutes?'

'Yes. It would be about that. I never read such a terribly complicated letter in all my life! All sorts of vulgar fractions and things, and percents . . . ' She laughed reflectively. 'I'd have had no need to do it at all if the postman hadn't mixed things up. He must have delivered the letter somewhere else because a man in plain-clothes whom Bella had never seen before brought it here and said it had been left at his house by mistake.'

Garth narrowed his eyes. In one move the provocative creature reclining on the divan had blown the postman angle sky high.

'Left elsewhere? And you don't know where?'

'Not the slightest idea, but I think it was awfully nice of the man to go to the trouble of bringing it. Most people would have pushed it in a letter box with 'not known at this address' written across it . . . '

'Mmmm . . . Yes indeed.'

Garth brought his attention back to the tea and finished both it and the bun. He was about to speak when the woman gushed again.

'More tea, Mr. Garth? And some more cake?'

'No, madam, really — ' Garth dived at a possibility, snatching out his cheroot case. 'I will smoke, though, if you have no objections?'

'Good heavens, no!' she laughed. 'I'm addicted to the vice myself, you know. I often think it is a pity women can't — or rather don't — smoke a pipe in public.'

Garth lighted a cheroot and felt happier. 'Did you know Granville Collins, madam?'

'Why, of course!' She seemed surprised that the fact should even be in doubt. 'He used to come here many a time. Likewise we used to see him often at his office.'

'Not his home?'

'No, for some reason he preferred to

keep his home life entirely to himself. After all, somebody or other did once say that an Englishman's home is his castle. Now who was it — ?'

Garth thumped his chest and muttered something about it not really mattering, as the woman fell to thought. She made him almost ashamed of growling out another question.

'What was your impression of him, Mrs. Morton? Was he good, bad, or indifferent?'

'Oh, he was *delightful*! Dudley and I knew him for many, many years and we saw very little change in him in all that time. He was the quiet, thoughtful type, so considerate in every way. Not that he was perfect, of course. No man is — or woman either. He had his little fads and faults, but had you known him I'm sure you'd have thought a nicer man could not have been met anywhere.'

Garth drew hard on his cheroot. 'Your husband said the same thing, but oddly enough various other acquaintances of Mr. Collins had a directly opposite opinion.'

'That,' Mrs. Morton replied indifferently, 'I can only attribute to plain jealousy. The great mass of people are usually jealous of a kindly man, are they not? It shows up their own faults so clearly.'

Garth reflected. In his mind was a picture of Beatrice Collins and the disaffection she had had for her husband. Less clear was the portrait of one Evelyn Drew who had hinted with singular lack of delicacy at some kind of 'intimacy'. On the one hand Collins was revealed as an unscrupulous immoralist; and on the other as a saint letting his light shine before men.

'Do have more tea, Mr. Garth! Your sitting there with no cup beside you makes me feel the most dreadful of hostesses.'

Mrs. Morton's effusive hospitality was having a smothering effect. Garth wanted to push her away with both hands, get some fresh air, and then hurl questions at her with complete disregard for her charm and sex. He smiled woodenly.

'I'm not a tea-drinking man, Mrs.

Morton, thanks all the same — but I would like to pester you a little further if I may. How long were your husband and you acquainted with Collins?'

'Oh — er — a long time.'

'Fifteen years?'

She made a bothered gesture. 'I really don't know. Is it so important?'

'It is to me, madam. We are working on a line of enquiry whereby we think that Mr. Collins was murdered because of something which happened in his life fifteen years ago. So naturally we want all the information we can get from people like you and Mr. Morton, who might have known him long ago.'

Garth had hoped to give the woman a jolt. Instead she merely looked blank.

'But would anybody wait fifteen years to — to exact some sort of revenge? To kill a man?'

'Some people,' Garth said deliberately, 'wait a lifetime!'

'Do they? How perfectly horrible!'

Garth was beginning to feel he was not getting anywhere, then he alerted as Mrs. Morton spoke again, abstractedly.

'I should imagine that Dudley and I did know Granville fifteen years ago — but time passes so quickly that it's hard to judge. I really can't understand it, Inspector. I'm sure he had no enemies. He was too nice a man.'

'Hmmm . . . Now for a personal question, Mrs. Morton, if I may. Your Christian name is 'Ruby', is it not?'

'Ruby?' She looked surprised. 'Why, no! And thank heaven it isn't; I don't like the names of jewels for girls. Mine's Hazel.'

'The devil it is!' Garth commented under his breath, then aloud: 'Really?'

Garth knew the M.O. record had referred to Vincent Darricourt's wife 'Ruby' being mixed up in the clothes cupboard affair. And records, even if incomplete, do not lie . . .

'You seem to doubt it, Inspector,' Hazel Morton remarked, still smiling at him, and getting to her feet. 'I'll tell you what I'll do. You must see my birth certificate — if you'll promise not to look at the year of birth!'

Garth grinned stiffly and rose with clumsy courtesy.

'Not that it really matters,' she added dryly. 'I'm forty-seven and not at all ashamed of it — '

'While you are about it,' Garth interrupted, 'would you let me see your marriage certificate as well? If you have it?'

'I've no need to, you know.' Her voice had challenge in it for a moment. 'Never mind though! I'll let you see it, I want you to find poor Granville's murderer just as much as you do yourself.'

She went gracefully from the room and Garth was agreeably satisfied at the smoothness of her hips and shoulders for forty-seven years of age. Speaking architecturally, she was in a fine state of preservation . . .

Garth glanced up at the maid as she came in for the tea-wagon, evidently having been instructed by her mistress to do so. In silence Garth resumed his seat, smoke wisping from his cheroot. He watched the woman at work for a moment or two then asked:

'Been with the Mortons long, Bella?'

She measured him, debating if she

should answer the question.

'Yes, sir,' she said finally. 'Twenty years.'

Garth saw her features more clearly now than in the dim light of the hall. They were flattish, somewhat pasty, with a large mouth. Redemption from the nondescript came in thoughtful, indeed intelligent, azurine eyes.

'Did your mistress telephone Mr. Morton yesterday morning between half past eight and nine, do you know?'

The maid hesitated. 'Am I compelled to answer that question, sir?'

'Not compelled.' Garth was studying her fixedly. 'I am just asking . . .'

Mrs. Morton came back into the room at that moment, oblong sheets of paper in her hand.

'The gentleman just asked me a question, m'm, and I don't know if you'd want me to answer it or not — '

'Oh, really?' Hazel Morton seemed engrossed in the forms she had brought. 'What was it?'

Garth repeated it stolidly, and Mrs. Morton laughed.

'Well, of course you can answer it, Bella. Don't be so silly! We want to help the Inspector, don't we?'

The maid regarded Garth stonily. 'Yes, sir. She was on the 'phone for fifteen minutes yesterday morning to the master . . . Will there be anything further?'

Garth shook his head and watched the woman as she pushed the wagon out noiselessly and closed the door. His eyes switched back to Mrs. Morton. She was seated sideways on the divan now, slender legs tucked under her and a perplexed look on her interesting face.

'I'm sorry if Bella seems a bit secretive, Inspector. It's just her way. She's really quite invaluable . . . She's a maid-cum-secretary, really. Does a lot of my husband's private correspondence. I daren't say too much to her, you understand — oh, here!' she broke off impatiently. 'I can never make head or tail of these official things. Read for yourself.'

He took the forms and read. One of them was a birth certificate; the other a marriage certificate. If the forms were the right ones two things were clear — Hazel Jackson had become Hazel Morton fifteen years before in December; and she had been born in Lincoln forty-seven years before, the daughter of Arthur Jackson, gunsmith, and Mildred Jackson, housewife.

'Mmmm . . . Thank you, Mrs. Morton. Everything quite in order. Tell me, did you ever hear of the name Darricourt?'

She shook her head. 'No — not as far as I can remember. Does it matter?'

'No, never mind. Incidentally, there's a little point I'm not quite clear on. The marriage certificate shows that you have been Mr. Morton's wife for fifteen years, but apparently your maid, Bella has been with you for twenty. There's a discrepancy somewhere.'

'Not really,' Hazel Morton said, folding up the forms and smiling. 'You see, she worked five years in my husband's home before he married me.'

Silence. Garth hesitated over something and he sensed for the second time that dim conviction of challenge.

He beamed genially and rose to his

feet. Then he sank back again as Mrs. Morton waved him down.

'But you can't go with things half finished like this, Mr. Garth!' she protested. 'I want you to see that awful letter I read to Dudley yesterday morning — '

'It doesn't really signify.'

'Oh but it does — !' She was fiddling among the cushions on the divan where the letter had apparently lodged itself, when she had brought it down with the forms. Then she whisked it up triumphantly — five sheets of it in single-spaced typing. Garth made a wry face and took it, began to glance through the lines. He did not pretend to understand one half of the quotations and figuring and finally handed it back.

'Thanks for letting me see it anyway, Mrs. Morton,' he said, rising up resolutely. 'I have the facts from your husband, of course. This letter, report, or whatever it is, was relayed to a Dictaphone, you know.'

She rose gracefully beside him and nodded, her blue eyes pensive.

'Yes — and I consider that was an awfully lucky chance since, unwittingly, it gives Dudley and me a perfect alibi! I mean, one could hardly be involved in the murder of poor Granville and telephoning at the same time, now could one?'

Garth smiled woodenly. 'No, madam — of course not. Well, thank you for the tea and the information. I'm sorry I butted in. Just happens to be my job . . . '

She followed him out into the hall, and laid a hand on his arm.

'Do come again, Inspector, if anything bothers you. I'm so anxious to help in every way I can — just as Dudley is. That's about all that friends can do when somebody is — murdered, is it not?'

'Indeed so, Mrs. Morton. Goodbye.'

Garth nodded and smiled, went off down the pathway and to his car. His smile was still there when he started up the engine but his colourless eyes could not have been less humourless . . .

16

Sergeant Whittaker had apparently just arrived back at the office and was on the point of settling at his desk to sort his notes as Garth entered.

'Six o'clock, sir, and you said to report back here. Can't do much more now since most of the shops are closing anyway.'

'Uh-huh.' Garth nodded and slung his hat up on the peg. 'How far did you get?'

'So far there doesn't seem to be anything we want — working from my memory of the wanted type that is. I covered three firms, and Calthorpe and Mason — they've got back too, by the way — covered seven between them. I've taken the type samples to Calligraphy and the particulars of each machine are on the sheets concerned. Knott said he'd let you have the information as soon as possible. Probably later on tonight or else tomorrow morning.'

'Mmmm . . . ' Garth took out a cheroot, and sat down in the swivel chair. His face broke into a grin. 'Suffering snakes, have I had a tough time of it with Mrs. Morton!'

'You managed to see her then?'

'I couldn't get out of the road of her! She's one of those cling-all-over-you type of women . . . Charming, mind you, but hell to interrogate.'

Garth gave Whittaker a brief resumé of the interview. At the end of it he was frowning and Garth was shrouded in blue haze.

'So that's the lay of the land, is it?' Whittaker mused. 'Instead of clearing anything up it adds to the mystery, doesn't it? How do we get round the postman problem? Was Mrs. Morton telling the truth, do you think?'

'Logically, I'd say why not? But being a suspicious sort of bloke at times — not all the time like you, Whitty — I'd say it's all lies. I'd go further, and say that Morton suddenly remembered we might check on the postman and telephoned his wife with that invention. The maid obviously knew what to say . . . ' Garth narrowed his eyes. 'Queer stick that maid! Hefty, phlegmatic type. Doesn't give anything away without permission, and none too freely even then. Don't like 'em Whitty.'

'No, sir — neither do I.'

Garth sighed. 'But I don't intend on adding more furrows to my forehead just because of that letter. There are other things quite as important. This 'Ruby' business, for one thing . . . '

'That I just don't understand, sir. Our records cannot be wrong in quoting one Ruby Darricourt as Darricourt's — Morton's — wife. The only answer to that one is that she showed you a faked birth certificate.'

Garth raised his colourless eyes.

'Why make things difficult? Showing me a faked birth certificate would be asking for it. She knows perfectly well that we can trace back from it to Somerset House — to her parents, and even if they are dead, records still speak. No, it is her own birth certificate all right. She's the daughter of Arthur Jackson, a Lincoln gunsmith . . . The solution to the problem is perfectly simple. Darricourt did marry one Ruby, then he either got divorced, Ruby died, or something, and Darricourt — now under the new name of Morton — married Hazel Jackson, the present wife, four months after the clothes cupboard affair. I was just about to ask if Morton had been married before, but I didn't want to show too much of my hand. I even thought of doing some fingerprint checking — then the whole thing became perfectly obvious to me. Second marriage! Simple!'

Whittaker gave a discreet cough.

'I admit it got me by the nose for a moment until I guessed it,' Garth said dryly. 'The description in the records would fit either woman. Evidently Morton likes the blue-eyed brown-haired type. In the morning I'll check with Somerset House re Ruby. If she's still alive she can be useful to us. As to other things — the following pointers stick in my mind. First — the maid knew that her mistress had 'phoned to Morton for fifteen minutes Why? A maid's place is in the kitchen, not listening to the exact length of time her mistress is telephoning, and a business call at that. Even if she does secretarial work for Morton that is no excuse. A slight point maybe, but worth mulling over —What else? Oh, yes! Mrs. Morton would insist on me reading the confounded letter that she had read to her husband. Why? She knew that I knew she'd read it, that her husband and maid had verified the fact, that a Dictaphone record had been made of it, yet she still wanted me to see the damned thing.'

'Gilding the lily, sir,' Whittaker said.

'Else the woman is so confoundedly pleasant she didn't want me to go without my being sure of everything. Charming woman! Twenty years ago she must have been a corker — Well,' Garth glanced at his watch, 'there are other things, too, but I want to think about 'em. In the meantime, I wonder what Pierce did to this office to fix up a microphone?'

As he looked about him keenly, the office door opened and Pierce came in.

'Never mind where it is,' he said calmly. 'It records perfectly — so mind your language, Mort! I heard everything you two just said. Under the desk edge there,' — he pointed — 'is the special bell push you wanted. Satisfied?'

Garth nodded blankly. 'Yes, I'm satisfied, but I'd like to know where — '

'No, that would never do. You might unconsciously look right at it and give the game away.'

With a grin the recording engineer went out and closed the door. Whittaker gave a shrug.

'Just what *is* the idea of it, sir?'

'You'll see in time; just playing one of my hunches.' Garth retrieved his trilby. 'More than this I refuse to do in one day. I've things to think about and a crossword puzzle to finish . . . You still haven't thought of a fresh four-letter word meaning 'brainless', I suppose?'

'Loon?' Whittaker suggested.

'No. Won't fit with the clue across. Well, I'm on my way. Stay if you want — '

'For another half hour, sir. I can finish typing the reports. The wife's away so I've nothing to hurry home for. 'Night, sir.'

★ ★ ★

240

Over the evening meal at home, which Garth and his still pretty, dark-haired wife had in comfort thanks to the three children being at the local sports tournament, Garth had little to say and, knowing his moods, his wife did not bother him.

When the meal was over he went into the room he used as his study and settled down in the easy chair beside a low-built series of shelves jammed with all manner of books, files, and general dust-collecting junk which had been a profound source of worry to his house-proud wife in all their years of married life.

'Got to be somewhere,' he muttered, as he pulled first one file down and then another, piling them on his knees. Heavy books followed.

Half an hour later, puzzled by the silence, his wife peeped in on him. He was in the easy chair absorbed in a newspaper-cutting file. Beside him, open at a page she could not read, was an omnibus volume of Ripley's *Believe It or Not*, a copy of Fowler's *Remarkable Accidents*, and a blue bound book of *Recent Advances in Forensic Medicine*.

'Would you like another cup of tea, dear?' Mrs. Garth asked softly.

'Eh?' Garth grinned and nodded. 'You bet I would! In fact I think we ought to make it champagne!'

'Whatever for?'

'Because of what I've found.' He slapped the books and then the newspaper-cutting file. 'You call all this stuff a dust-collection — maybe it is, but it is also our bread and butter. Collecting facts and strange anecdotes, m'dear, helps a plodding policeman like me to keep his job . . . You know I'm working on the Collins case?'

'Yes, dear. I read newspapers, too. Collins was shot in a locked office with nobody ever going near him, wasn't he?'

'Right! And I've just worked out how it was done! It's the only conceivable explanation . . . ' Garth got to his feet actively.

'Where's that telephone? I've got to see Dr. Myers first thing tomorrow . . . '

★ ★ ★

At nine-thirty the following morning, presaged by his telephone call, Garth was

242

in Dr. Myers' city surgery. The GP didn't look particularly pleased, either. Apart from his work for the Yard he had a busy practice to attend to.

'What's it all about, Garth?' he asked, puzzled by the Inspector's bland grin. 'I've already let you have my report on Collins — '

Garth settled in a chair by the desk and crossed his legs. 'All I want to know from you is — are you sure you didn't err in your diagnosis of how Collins died?'

Myers' eyebrows shot up. 'Great Scott, man, what do you take me for? I've a reputation to maintain.'

'You told me over the 'phone you had taken X-ray plates of the wound which caused death.'

Myers nodded and looked grim. From his filing cabinet he handed them across and Garth held them to the light of the window. Myers' forefinger began to trace upon them.

'There you are — before I took the bullet out. You can see it lodging at the top of the heart there, just below the area of the pulmonary veins.'

'Mmmm . . . ' Garth mused. 'Is it not a fact that a direct wound to the heart doesn't spill much blood?'

'That's right. Not much to see around the wound itself. There wasn't, anyway. What are you getting at?'

'Just satisfying myself. Look, Doctor . . . ' Garth laid the plates aside. 'Are you convinced from the position of the bullet that instant death would have occurred?'

Myers nodded. 'Considering everything, yes; as I said in the report. You notice where it is lodging? In case you can't read an X-ray plate very well — being a non-professional — let me tell you that the bullet pierced the top of the heart which by all medical laws must have stopped its action . . . Yes, I know heart wounds can take place and instant death does not result, but in this case it would be inevitable.'

'Suppose it had been a fraction higher, and hadn't lodged at the top of his heart? Would he have died then?'

'But it *did*!' Myers protested. 'And it killed him. And if it hadn't it would have been in the muscular tissue and he'd very probably have still died, though not instantaneously. A highly delicate operation might even have saved him. This, though, is a waste of time. Bullets don't go in jerks, Garth: they go to their target and only stop when they get there.'

'This one pursued an erratic course, I think you said?'

'In a way. It didn't travel in a straight line, by any means. There is no possible doubt about the fact that it was shot from above, but inside the body the tissue obstruction made it take a slightly curved path. It entered just above the heart and finished up in the top of the heart itself. Hardly pierced it, but it was enough to stop its action.'

Garth got to his feet. 'Thanks, Doc — you know your job. But it doesn't pay sometimes to be too hidebound. Imagination helps, you know ... Incidentally, Colonel Fordyce is playing hell about you judging the shot as having come from fifteen feet. He seems to think it's impossible to judge the exact distance beyond it being long or short.'

'I said 'approximately',' Myers observed sourly. 'I know the muzzle velocity of a thirty-eight, and I know the normal resistance of human tissue. If it had come from any nearer it would have penetrated much further into the body; if from any farther away it wouldn't have gone in so deeply. Only a private deduction and not intended to be accurate. I did it as a rough help for you.'

'Thanks, Doc — and don't ever say that in front of Colonel Fordyce!'

Garth left the surgery and continued on his way to Scotland Yard. When he got into the office he found it empty. On the blotter were the neatly typed statements to date, part of Whittaker's duty as secretary; and a note from him observing that he had resumed his investigation re Valiant Typewriters at 9.10 a.m.

'Good old Whitty!' Garth murmured, throwing his hat on the peg and then settling in his chair at the desk. He sat thinking for a moment, then reached for the telephone.

His first call was to Somerset House. Twenty minutes later he had a note on his scratchpad that said that Ruby Darricourt had died in a London nursing home from pneumonia on August 20th, fifteen years ago . . . Next he got through to Dudley Morton.

'Ah Mr. Morton! I'm afraid I'm bothering you again. I'd rather like a few words with you if you'd come over to my office.

'If you wish,' Morton's quiet voice assented. 'But I find it annoying to keep getting my business interrupted in this fashion. However — I'll be there in fifteen minutes.'

'Much obliged.'

Putting the instrument down Garth picked up the reports Whittaker had typed, began sorting through them. Among them was the latest from the Calligraphy Department. So far, the wanted typewriter had not been located. None of the types to date matched that on the warning note . . . Then there were the statements of Andrew Martin, Mary Baxter, the janitor, Evelyn Drew — Garth had got this far, cheroot burned down to the stub, when there was a knock on the

247

door and a constable showed in the immaculate stockbroker.

'Good of you to come, sir.' Garth got up and shook hands. 'Take a seat. Cigarette? Cheroot?'

Dudley Morton put his grey hat carefully on the desk and sat down. He took a cigarette without speaking and lighted it

Garth settled at his desk again and stubbed out his cheroot in the ashtray, pressing the bell-button under the desk edge with his other hand. Then he sat back and aimed cold eyes across the desk.

'There are one or two little things which have cropped up, Mr. Morton, that you may wish to explain without me taking the obvious way of finding them out. First, your employment of Granville Collins fifteen years ago as your head clerk.'

Dudley Morton did not seem to be in the least disturbed. Instead he gave that peculiar smile which only seemed to involve his top lip.

'You're surely not making a mystery out of *that*, Inspector?'

'I'm not — but you seem to be, otherwise you'd have mentioned it yesterday.'

'I'm afraid I would *never* have mentioned it if you hadn't have called it to my notice. It's such a trivial thing . . . Of course I employed him. That was how I first met him, how we became such firm friends. It was partly his skill that made my business so prosperous. That is why I kept him in tow when he branched off in business on his own.'

'After the 'Clothes Cupboard Mystery' you mean?'

Morton reflected, then reached out to the brass tray and knocked cigarette ash into it. Garth grinned abruptly and got to his feet.

'Have a brandy and soda, Mr. Morton? I often do for my dyspepsia. You might care for one too — but not for dyspepsia.'

'Thanks,' Morton said briefly. 'With plenty of soda, please.'

Garth fixed up two glasses and brought them over on a small tray. Morton took one and Garth went back with his own glass to his swivel chair.

'Well, you've had a fighting chance to think about things, Mr. Morton. What about it? You're not going to try and deny you were Vincent Darricourt at that time, I hope?'

'No, I don't deny it. It isn't necessary. But I do deny your right to question me about it. As far as the 'Clothes Cupboard' business is concerned I had nothing to do with it, and the police released me. You should know that. After all, it was you who picked me up!'

'You remember that, then?' Garth asked, after he had drained his glass. 'We both moved a bit faster in those days, eh?'

'I'm not sitting here to exchanging jocular anecdotes of our youth, Inspector! I'd remind you that the police released me on the grounds of insufficient evidence, so there is nothing more you can do about it.'

'No? You have your facts twisted.' Garth's face set into malevolent hardness. 'You never got as far as court — nor your wife Ruby. You didn't get to a trial and get yourself acquitted, whereby nothing could ever be proved against you afterward. You were simply released because of insufficient evidence. The case was closed . . . but only for the time being.'

'You surely don't propose to rake it all up again now?' Morton snapped.

'That depends. I believe the murder of Granville Collins and the death of that woman in your home are closely interwoven, that one is the key to the other — and I shall go on making a nuisance of myself until I have proved it.'

Morton put his finished glass on the desk deliberately, and sat contemplating it.

'You changed your name after the 'Clothes Cupboard' business to sidetrack any chance of scandal, didn't you?' Garth asked. 'Not only because it would have spoiled your business activities — for an affair like that could have made a terrible odour — but also because you had fallen in love with one Hazel Jackson. She, ambitious for social progress, was unobtainable while there was a dirty smear on your record, and so a complete change of personality became necessary. I'll hazard that you had your normal crooked teeth removed and the screw-type put in their place; that you bleached your hair to blonde, which today, with greyness coming into it, gives it its silvery sheen; that you changed the parting to the side, shaved off your dark moustache, and so became Dudley Morton without benefit of Deed Poll. You then moved from Hampstead to Kensington, and by some means best known to yourself got your finances under the control of your new name — you can have as many names as you want in a bank account anyway — and so restarted as Dudley Morton . . . Am I right?'

Morton reflected, his eyes on Garth's harsh, emaciated face. Then he shrugged.

'Yes, it's right . . . To have changed my name legally and retained my normal appearance would have served no useful purpose whatever. I decided to cut everything out, transfer my finances — which I did while I was still Vincent Darricourt — and then I took on a new identity. My wife died from pnuemonia about a week after we had been in the hands of the police.'

'I know. I checked on that with Somerset House.'

'You did, eh?' Morton gave a cynical smile. 'Well, it was my present wife who insisted I make the change before she would consent to marry me.'

'You were fortunate in discovering a second wife so quickly,' Garth commented coldly.

'I'd known Hazel Jackson for years!' Morton retorted.

'Had you, though?' Garth fingered his jaw. 'As far as I can see, then, you changed your identity and got away with it, except for one person — Granville Collins. He knew you as Darricourt, obviously, and he knew you as Morton. He must have done because of that 'retainer fee' business.'

'He,' Morton replied warily, 'was one man I never kept out of my confidence. He knew too much about stocks for that.'

'And about . . . other things?' Garth suggested.

'I don't know what you mean.' Morton stubbed his cigarette in the ashtray deliberately.

The office was intensely quiet for a moment or two, then:

'Look here, Inspector, I know it's your job to probe the death of Collins to the depths, and to cross-examine all his acquaintances — close and distant. But the fact remains that with all the jugglings and contortions in the world you cannot evade one fact: At the time Collins met his death I was in my office with plenty of witnesses to testify to it, and my wife was talking to me on the 'phone — though I can assure you that she had nothing to do with it, anyway. Those things can't be altered, Inspector, and I don't see why I should answer any more of these questions. I've been too frank for my own good perhaps — but it's only because I liked Collins and want to help you.'

Garth rose to his feet, smiling rather fixedly.

'And I appreciate it, Mr. Morton. Sorry I bothered you, but I had to clear up the mists about Darricourt and Morton. You understand?'

Morton rose and retrieved his hat. 'I suppose I have to,' he answered grimly.

'Now if you'll excuse me I have a good deal of business to attend to. Good morning, Inspector.'

Garth held the door open for him and closed it slowly when Morton had gone into the corridor. Then, going over to the empty glass Morton had used he straddled his fingers inside it and walked with it to Fingerprints, where he ordered it to be checked with the prints of Vincent Darricourt. This off his mind he returned to the office, just as the interphone buzzed. It was the voice of Chief Radio Engineer Pierce.

'We got the whole conversation, Mortimer. What do you want done with it?'

'File it, 'til I'm ready,' Garth replied briefly. 'Thanks.' He switched off, frowned, then pulled the scratchpad to him and began writing. It was his favourite way of sorting out the ideas running through his mind.

Granville Collins shot in his office with nobody near to him. Conclusions (Theoretical): Death occurred in the office — since he was seen to enter the

office, but the wound occurred elsewhere. Co-relation between the two
points needed.

Possible focal point of shot — Back
Mercer Street roof. Only evidence — A
.38 revolver that fired the bullet that
killed Collins. Possible people who
fired the gun: Dudley Morton (alibi
strong); Hazel Morton (alibi strong);
Bella the maid (no alibi); Andrew
Martin (concrete alibi); Beatrice Collins (no alibi); Derek Collins (no alibi);
Evelyn Drew (no alibi); Howard
Farrow (no alibi, though he had
undoubted reason for being in the
neighbourhood); Janitor (out of reckoning).

Motives?

Dudley Morton — to eliminate the
payment of hush money? Why, if he is
as wealthy as he appears? One thousand pounds a month would be a small
price to pay for silence and far safer
than risking possible murder. Suggestion: That Morton is in hard straits
financially. Angle: Granville Collins
told his wife that he would soon be

moving to better things. This suggests he knew of a forthcoming extra source of money, as he thought. Conclusion: That he highered his demands to Morton but got shot instead of achieving his aim.

Hazel Morton — This may tie up with her husband. What affects him should affect her. Seems very sure that the Dictaphone recording provides a perfect alibi. Why? Is it over-eagerness on her part or just spontaneity of nature?

Mary Baxter. None that is obvious.
Andrew Martin. None that is obvious.
Beatrice Collins. Very strong.
Derek Collins. Very strong.
Howard Farrow. None, but might see if there is one.
Evelyn Drew. Plenty. Raw deal in her youth.
Bella. None visible, but twenty years might have produced one.

Garth scowled at the notes, a parade of the various personalities marching through his mind. Andrew Martin with his full moon blandness; he might have had a motive but certainly not much opportunity. He had never gone out of the building. Mary Baxter with her faint in the office when she had got out of her chair after seeing the body lying under the window . . . Garth paused for a moment in his thoughts, brooding over the recollection. A small possibility lurked there — that Mary Baxter had definitely been amazed at finding Collins in the office, and dead too.

'Hmmm — maybe,' he grunted, and resumed his meditations.

Evelyn Drew with her hard, faded features and a fifteen-year-old grudge; Howard Farrow with his impudent face and up-standing hair; Dudley Morton, always smiling with his top lip and with eyes so placid you couldn't tell what lay behind them. Mrs. Collins, admitting her likes and dislikes with complete openness and with few guiding expressions on her small features; Mrs. Morton with her gushing amiability and enormous sense of hospitality . . .

'Damn!' Garth muttered. 'Every one of

'em, even to that maid Bella, reacts exactly as you'd expect. Seems I've left too many holes even yet. More checking up to be done . . . '

17

Garth went downstairs to his car and finished up at 45 Darlington Road, South Norwood. He sat surveying the house for a while. It was of the good middle class semi-detached variety, with leaded light windows and pale mauve curtains. Mary Baxter had hinted that her parents were not without money, and such indeed was apparently the case.

Garth rang the bell. A tall, blonde woman of obvious style opened the door. Her polished hair was piled in ringlets, her lips and cheeks were made up, though without delicacy. She raised pencilled eyebrows.

'Inspector Garth, madam — Scotland Yard,' Garth displayed his warrant card and recollection dawned in the woman's eyes.

'Oh, yes! Won't you come in, Inspector?' She showed him into a well-furnished drawing room and he settled in an armchair.

'Did you want to see my daughter?' she enquired, her face troubled. 'As a matter of fact she's out at the moment, looking for a new post. Not that I approve.'

The woman took up a stand beside the mantelpiece, sideways so that one smooth hip bulged outwards and one elbow lay on the edge of the mahogany shelf.

'It isn't essential that I see your daughter, madam,' Garth replied, shrugging. 'This is merely a routine call. Sergeant Whittaker rang you up yesterday, I believe?'

'Yes — or somebody did, and asked me if Mary overslept on the morning her employer was — shot. She did, of course. I had to awaken her.'

'That is what interests me. What time did you awaken her?'

'It was about nine-twenty. Usually she is awake at ten past eight.'

'That was a long time to wait, madam, wasn't it?'

Mrs. Baxter smiled faintly. 'Matter of fact I wasn't awake myself until nine o'clock. You see, I'm a nightclub receptionist and as a rule I don't get home until the small hours. Normally I leave it to Mary to awaken me — but this time the position was reversed. My husband is away a great deal; he's a supervisor in the scientific testing department of the railway — testing rails and things — and he's often busy in various parts of the country on that account.'

'I see. Then, I take it, Mary had breakfast and dashed off to business?'

'Yes. She left here at twenty to ten.'

'Arriving at the office about ten,' Garth mused. 'Yes, that's about right from here. I believe, from what your daughter told me, that you didn't approve of her working for Mr. Collins?'

'I certainly did not! Nor did my husband either. Not because of anything wrong with Mr. Collins — I hardly knew anything about him except that he had queer habits — but because Mary has absolutely no need to go out and work. Not that sort of work, anyway. She is capable of much better things than office secretary. She's an excellent pianist, has a good voice, can dance perfectly — her life should be theatrical, but she just doesn't want it. She's at an age to please herself and there is nothing I can do about it.'

Garth got to his feet, smiling. 'Well, Mrs. Baxter, I shan't need to take up any more of your time. Many thanks. Just a check up you know.'

She saw him to the front door and he went down the path to his car, and for a while sat musing. Finally he glanced at his watch and it showed 11.15. This decided him and he drove back to the Yard to find Sergeant Whittaker had returned to the office.

' 'Morning, sir . . . ' He looked up from his own desk. 'I've got something to report — that's why I'm back. I've tracked one of the sources of the Dampdew Parchment, and it may be significant.'

'Good!' Garth threw his hat on the peg. 'Well, let's have it.'

'Twenty-four reams of Dampdew Parchment were bought recently by the firm of Thorne and Buckster, the grain merchants, of 89, Wharf Street, East Central.'

Garth settled at the desk and tugged out his cheroot case. 'The firm employing

Evelyn Drew, eh?'

'Yes, sir!' Sergeant Whittaker positively shone with pride.

'And that's as far as you've got?'

'Up to now. I've got the various retailers going through their invoices and it's a long job. I'm hoping for more luck this afternoon. After all, sir, Miss Drew is suspect, isn't she?'

'Oh, surely,' Garth agreed. 'As is Mary Baxter, and Uncle Tom Cobleigh and all. It's interesting, Whitty, but I wouldn't say more than that. There is nothing remarkable in a business firm buying in twenty-four reams of good quarto paper even if they do employ Evelyn Drew. I'll bear it in mind, anyway. What does signify is that blasted typewriter. Once we know where that is we can really get somewhere.'

'Yes, sir . . . but you'll remember Miss Drew refused to give an alibi. That's pretty bad, to my mind.'

'Mebbe she was just being awkward. She's the type.'

Whittaker glanced down at the desk and picked up a report. 'This came in from Dabs while you were out, sir.'

Garth took the card and glanced over the statement upon it . . .

Glass submitted for inspection contains fingerprints that in 20 major points check with those of Vincent Darricourt, already recorded.

'Bang goes number one of your objections, Whitty,' Garth grinned, as he tossed the card down. 'I had Morton here while you were out and gave him a drink to get his prints on the glass. Now we *know* that Morton is Darricourt. Fingerprints never change, thank God, whatever else might. I got a full statement out of him, by the way, and had it recorded. You won't need to take it down until later.'

'Sorry I missed that,' Whittaker sighed. 'What did he say?'

'He was damned frank — either because he's genuine or because he thought he'd seem so by admitting everything. Or mebbe it was the apparent absence of witnesses that made him bold . . . ' Garth settled in his chair and went briefly over the details.

'Trouble is,' Whittaker said, when it was over, 'that he's right, sir. That alibi of his — and his wife's too for that matter — they're cast iron and we can't prove otherwise.'

'Hmmm — mebbe.' Garth did not pursue the point. 'Incidentally, I also dropped in on Mary Baxter's mother. Her father is away somewhere.'

Whittaker listened once again to details, and a look of suspicious wonder came into his eyes.

'Suppose,' he said, 'Mary Baxter had something to do with it? That is, ignoring the problem of how Collins was found dead in his office. That point hasn't been cleared up yet.'

'But it has,' Garth said blandly. 'I solved it last night and verified it this morning. I know exactly how Collins died . . . But go on, Whitty. Sorry!'

'*Go on!* You expect me to do that when you've found out how Collins was murdered? How was it done, sir?'

Garth sighed. 'It's perfectly simple, really, like the five matchboxes turned out to be. All I can suggest at the moment is that you read Fowler's *Strange Accidents* and Ripley's *Believe It or Not* — you can get both from the library — and tell me what you think about the case of Jonathan Strande in the former and Shineas Gage in the latter. Then there are the cases of Beatrice Smith and Mason Berney for good measure . . . If you haven't got the answer after sorting out the first two names — the latter two being in news-cutting form and unavailable to you — then I'm sorry for you.'

'You could save me an awful lot of headache, sir, if you tell me.'

Garth grinned, 'You want promotion, don't you? Work things out for yourself, my bonny boy. It's the best way . . . But you were saying about Mary Baxter?'

Whittaker frowned. 'Look here, can I safely assume that Collins was shot elsewhere than in his office?'

'You certainly can!'

'And you say Mrs. Baxter slept later than usual? Than *usual*, sir! That is significant: she may have been drugged! As I see it, sir, Mary usually wakes her mother up. Now let's suppose — only *suppose*, mind you — that she left something about the night before which her mother would be bound to use. Say a cup or glass or something for a drink before going to bed. In it was a sleeping-draught. Mary, though, was up and about early, knew her mother would stay asleep for a long time, and off she went and killed Collins — somewhere. Then she came back home and went to bed, staying there with an 'oversleeping' story until her mother woke up and aroused her.'

Garth blew out a cloud of smoke.

'It *could* be done, sir,' Whittaker insisted. 'Nothing easier.'

'Sure; I thought of that,' Garth agreed. 'But *why*?'

'That we don't know. But who knows what — er — intrigue, what intimacy, developed between that girl and Collins in the six months she worked for him? We already know from Evelyn Drew that he was inclined towards that kind of thing, so I can't see why he shouldn't still be that way with Mary Baxter. A man's never too old, if I may say so. She might have had a very good reason for wanting to wipe him out.'

'So she went and bought a thirty-eight and did the deed, eh?'

'Maybe it's her father's.'

'Or her grandfather's,' Garth said heavily. 'And, of course, it was essential that she type a note to Scotland Yard telling everybody what was going to happen.'

'Why not, sir? Calligraphy says that the note was typed by an expert. Well, Mary Baxter is an expert typist. Then again, criminals often plank themselves right in the open for the sheer object of deflecting suspicion.'

Garth shook his head. 'Like hell they do, Whitty. You study criminal records and you'll find that that is about the last thing they do. It's about as big a fallacy as the one about the criminal always returning to the scene of the crime. That only happens about once in a thousand times, and then it is only to pick up something inadvertently left behind. And the note said that Collins would be shot *in his office*, remember! Why, if Mary Baxter did it, did she say that when she intended to commit the murder elsewhere?'

Whittaker was breathing hard, obviously still determined not to be outdone.

'It was to . . . distract attention!' he snapped his fingers. 'That's it! To lead the police to the office and away from the scene of the crime. That's why she fainted. She was so staggered to find he had died in his office after all that she went out like a puffed candle flame.'

'Correct,' Garth agreed calmly, and transferred his cheroot to the other side of his mouth.

Whittaker gave a start. 'You — you mean you think I'm right?'

'About the note you are — yes. I tumbled to that angle some time ago. The murderer did not send it out of a sense of ego. You will remember that a fixed time for the murder was given — between nine and nine-thirty, more or less assuring that attention by the police would — for about half an hour anyway — be diverted from the real spot. It was done deliberately to distract our attention, That Collins finished up in his office and *did* die there is, I'll wager, something that is baffling the killer to the point of insanity at this moment. It was one of those monstrous slices of good luck that Fate sometimes hands out willy-nilly to a wrongdoer. The impossible — seemingly — happened.'

'Then you admit it must be Mary Baxter?'

'Why should I?' Garth studied the notes on his desk again. 'If she fainted from the shock of seeing Collins, why did she wait ten minutes to do it? We saw her after she'd been in the office looking at the body for quite that long, remember. Why didn't she pass out right away?'

'Latent reaction, maybe. Women are funny that way.' Whittaker did not sound at all sure of himself.

Garth gave a sour look that sent Whittaker back to his desk to do some more typing and, in between times, some silent meditation.

For a while there was only the faint clicking of Whittaker's noiseless machine and the rustle of papers, then at last

Garth banged his cheroot in the ashtray irritably.

'Damn me, I'm running into a brick wall every time I think about this clothes cupboard business. Look here, Whitty, if you were wealthy — would you go around in a suit with grass stains on it, no matter how slight they might be?'

Whittaker looked blank.

'It's a simple question,' Garth said impatiently. 'With all due respect to my late superior, he missed something — and I think it was slight grass stains. Where do you pick 'em up usually?'

'Sitting in the grass,' Whittaker replied, with inhuman logic.

'Or lying in it,' Garth got up and retrieved his hat. 'I'm going to grab some lunch and then have another chat with Mrs. Collins.'

At half-past two Garth was ringing the bell of the Collins house. As on the previous occasion it was the poker-faced Milly who opened the door to him. This time she did not even question his business or identity but showed him into the familiar drawing room.

Garth stood beside the window, hands clasped behind him and his lips tight. There was a multitude of small but vital threads weaving through his brain.

'Good afternoon, Mr. Garth . . . '

Beatrice Collins had come in quietly, dressed in dead black. She looked paler than on his previous visit and her dark eyes seemed larger. They surveyed him with a mixture of welcome and anxiety.

'I hope there's nothing wrong with Derek again?' she asked, motioning to a chair.

Garth shook his head and settled down opposite her. 'No, madam — nothing like that. That young man is right out of the reckoning, rest assured. This time I'm afraid I'm going to have to bother you. I've made progress — good progress — but to fit some of the parts of this jigsaw into place it's necessary to delve back quite a good way.'

Beatrice Collins looked at him in cool interest. Sensitive to the slightest reaction of the people whom he questioned, he could feel she was putting up her defences. She gave a needless tug at the hem of her skirt.

'A good way, Mr. Garth?'

'Fifteen years at least. You mentioned that you had been married sixteen years.'

'Yes — which is correct.'

'I see.' Garth edged himself forward. 'You also told me that your husband always kept a revolver beside him — the thirty-eight — for protection against burglary — '

'Yes! Yes, he did!' Emotion abruptly coloured the pale cheeks. An indignant sparkle came into the brown eyes. 'Surely you don't doubt my word?'

'Of course not, madam,' Garth smiled gravely. 'I would merely like to know when this habit of having a revolver at the bedside developed. You told me it began shortly after you were married. You would help me a lot if you could remember the exact time.' Garth sat back in resolute calm. 'Don't hurry yourself, Mrs. Collins: just let your memory have its head.'

She frowned hard at her shoes and began to bite her underlip gently. Suddenly she looked up. 'I believe it would be about a year after we were married. He never used to do such a thing during the first year of our marriage; then all of a sudden he seemed to develop this peculiar suspicion of burglars, or maybe enemies. That was when he bought the gun.'

'Mmmm — fifteen years ago. I'll make a guess, Mrs. Collins. He started the habit in August of that year.'

'Why, yes!' She looked startled. 'It *was* August! It comes back to me now. One very hot night when we found it difficult to sleep I happened to see him putting the gun under his pillow . . . that was after he had fastened his key ring to the mattress wire as usual. It was the first time I'd ever seen the revolver. Naturally, I was alarmed and wanted to know the reason.

'Then' — she gestured quickly — 'he told me all about his fear of burglaries and so forth. After that he kept the gun in full view since it didn't matter any more if I saw it. But I'm sure he never had it before that time. Mr. Garth, how could you possibly have known when it was?'

'Trade secret,' Garth answered, grinning. 'I'm glad you've verified it. Tell me something else. Was there any distinct change in your husband's character from that time onwards? Was that when the first signs of a rift began to appear?'

'No, it was years afterwards before open dissension showed itself. He was, of course, always strangely moody and erratic even before I married him, which fact you have yourself explained away as claustrophobia. That is, there was no startling change in him after he began keeping a revolver at his bedside. He did seem to become somewhat furtive, though, as if he were always afraid something were going to happen to him.'

'I see . . . '

Mrs. Collins stirred. 'You must have a cup of tea, Inspector — '

'No, madam!' Garth shook his head, full of the memories of his antics at the hands of Mrs. Morton. 'I've only just had lunch . . . Was your husband's tendency against having a car always present, right from the time you first knew him?'

'No; that developed later. Even then he

276

wouldn't have objected to an open car — but I don't like them, and so between us we didn't have a car at all. That is, I haven't liked them of later years. When we first got married he used to have a small two-seater with one of those folding roofs. I think I mentioned that to you, didn't I?'

A faint gleam came into Garth's eyes. 'That is a point which interests me immensely. Travelling in an open car evidently did not seem to be a 'shut in' arrangement. I think I'm right in saying, Mrs. Collins, that one August evening, fifteen years ago, he was out in that two-seater having gone to keep a business appointment with one Vincent Darricourt. He didn't return home until about three in the morning, did he?'

'I don't know how you know these things,' she said quietly, 'but you're quite right. I shan't forget it for one very good reason. The police were here next day. There was some horrible business, connected with his employer Darricourt, I mean. A woman was found murdered in Mr. Darricourt's home and — and Gran was cross-examined as to his movements the night before. Fortunately he was able to sound convincing.'

'The dead woman was, of course, Miss Beryl Cleveland, a wealthy recluse.'

Garth waved a hand gently as Beatrice Collins opened her month to speak. 'I know all about it, or at any rate I know the bare details. Since, unfortunately I cannot question your husband I am resorting to you. Can you tell me what he really did on that night when he came home so late?'

'Even though it was fifteen years ago, Mr. Garth, I can more or less remember this incident because, as I say, of the unpleasantness which followed it. Gran told me at teatime — that is about seven o'clock when he got in from the office — that he had suddenly remembered some important business he had to report immediately to his employer, Mr. Darricourt. He said he'd hop round there straight away in the car as they — Mr. Darricourt and his wife — were going away for a brief holiday to their cottage in Sussex.'

'Uh-huh. Then what?'

'I just don't know — ' Mrs. Collins's cheeks were deathly pale again under the remorseless eyes. 'He left here at about half past seven and didn't return until three in the morning.'

'Then he was away from home for an unprecedented length of time since Darricourt only lived in Hampstead and you lived here, as now. In a car your husband could soon have covered the distance. Weren't you — alarmed?'

'Not really. When involved in a business conference with Mr. Darricourt, there were times when my husband had been away for even longer. I simply assumed that he and Darricourt were discussing something most important before Darricourt went away. So I went to bed as usual.'

'And then?'

'His coming home awakened me.' Beatrice Collins looked uncomfortable. 'Then he told me that he'd never even seen Darricourt. He'd found that the Darricourts had already left for Sussex. He'd started out after them in his car, only for it to break down in the country,

279

miles from anywhere. He'd spent the rest of the time repairing it.'

A beatific smile spread slowly over Garth's grim features. 'Ah, I see. So that was the story he told you. What did you think of it?'

'I believed it, of course,' she replied coldly. 'And I still believed it when I found we were involved with the police next day. I shall go on believing it — always.'

'That's only natural, and I respect you for it. Loyalty to your husband's memory — good enough. I take it you knew Darricourt and his wife Ruby?'

'I'd met them once or twice. I cannot say that I was much impressed by either of them. I was glad when Darricourt gave up business — after the Beryl Cleveland affair — and Gran started in business on his own.'

'Mmmm . . . When your husband did start on his own did he happen to mention the fact that he had come into unexpected money?'

Beatrice Collins shook her head. 'He never used to tell me how much he earned, or how he earned it — except that I knew it was in stocks and shares. As I told you before, he was always promising to do a lot and never doing it. It was galling to me, but for the boy's sake I stuck beside him and hoped for a change one day. I really do believe he meant to do something big this last time only . . . Well, we know what happened.'

'Only too well,' Garth admitted quietly. 'And, if I remember aright, you have never met a man named Dudley Morton?'

'No.' She shrugged. 'But I've heard of him at times in the newspapers. He's a broker in the City, isn't he? I expect Gran would have known him.'

'Yes . . . ' Garth looked round the quiet, well-furnished room absently.

In the ensuing silence the woman looked at him in vague wonder, not unmixed with suspicion.

'Do you think, Inspector, that my husband . . . murdered Beryl Cleveland?' The words were spoken deliberately: evidently Beatrice Collins had thought them out carefully before uttering them.

'I am not paid to say what I think, madam — only what I know. I draw conclusions, as you do yourself.'

'But why can't you say?' she insisted emotionally. 'Gran's dead, isn't he? What difference can it make if he did? He's beyond the law now.'

'Yes, but you aren't,' Garth pointed out. 'Don't you find the publicity concerning the murder of your husband unpleasant enough, without the prospect of him being a murderer himself added to it? Don't forget that a good deal of dirt will come out at the inquest, too.'

'I would rather know,' she said quietly. 'I haven't exactly been taking things as they come since my husband was murdered, Inspector. I've done a great deal of thinking as to the reason for it and whom might have done it. Would you like me to tell you what I believe? Unofficially that is. You won't use it against me? I haven't any proof, you see . . .'

'I'm sorry, madam, but I can't promise anything. I'm a police officer, interested in whatever evidence I can get. I can only respect your confidence in so far as I consider certain things are irrelevant to the case. If you care to take the risk — '

She hesitated, then nodded her dark head firmly.

'I don't think that my husband actually murdered that woman Beryl Cleveland, but I do think that circumstances may have forced him somehow to — to kill her. I don't know, and never shall. I think that maybe that happened, and that some relative of hers has been waiting all these years to get their revenge and so shot my husband — cleverly, ingeniously, so no trace could ever show.' She shrugged slightly. 'Naturally, I don't pretend to know how that woman's body got into the clothes cupboard in the Darricourt home, nor do I know how my husband was shot dead and nobody ever seen as the culprit.'

'Mmm — well, it's a very brave attempt, madam, though there are a good few inconsistencies in it, invisible to the naked eye. What I am wondering is this: It will probably sound an odd thing, but do you know if your husband carried something about him that was extremely secret? Say, something like a piece of paper, well hidden. Did he ever mention anything like that, or did you see anything of that kind at any time when perhaps repairing his clothes or sewing on buttons?'

'No, never. And I just can't imagine what you mean . . . '

Garth smiled grimly and got to his feet. She rose too and their eyes met. 'I'm perhaps on the wrong horse there,' he admitted, reaching for his hat on the chair arm. 'Just one of those little hunches I get sometimes . . . However, you have told me things this afternoon, Mrs. Collins, which have done a great deal to clear the air. When a problem goes back fifteen years as this one does it demands pretty well of research, memory, and co-operation on the part of those concerned.'

'If I think of anything else,' she said, walking thoughtfully with him through the doorway into the hall, 'I'll let you know right away.'

'I'd be glad.' Garth grinned genially. 'The boy been catching any more butterflies?'

'I don't think he ever will again, Mr.

Garth.' She shook hands, then watched Garth's back as he went down the pathway to his car. He eased himself under the steering wheel, dragged out a cheroot and lighted it thankfully.

'Mmmm — so far, so good,' he muttered. 'Bit by bit the dirt is being shovelled away . . . '

18

It was half past three when he arrived back at Scotland Yard. Calthorpe was seated in the hide armchair by the doorway, talking with Whittaker as he typed.

'Well, Calthorpe, anything fresh?' Garth gave the PC man an expectant glance.

'Yes sir. I've tracked down a consignment of Dampdew Parchment to the firm of Dudley Morton, stock and share broker. He bought it about three weeks ago on the strength of traveller's samples. Twelve reams for a trial.'

Garth took a deep pull at his cheroot and went over to the window. 'Morton, eh? Good!'

'I've also brought in the last lot of typing samples,' Calthorpe went on. 'Mason and I have been to everybody having a Valiant typewriter — and some job that was! We've got samples of the lot. I turned them over to Calligraphy and they're on with the tests now.'

'Excellent,' Garth commented. 'See what happens next, then there's a new line I want you to get on. Find out — by any means you care to use and with whatever boys you need to help you — just what state the finances of Dudley Morton are in. Get to know with whom he banks, what he's worth, how his business is going on — everything. Understand? You've got your authority for probing. Do it discreetly.'

Calthorpe nodded imperturbably. 'Right, sir, I'll go to work on it right away. I think Mason and Pascal will be enough to help me . . . ' He paused in the doorway. 'By the way, Chief, have you fathomed out yet how Collins got killed? I was one of the chaps who was watching the building and saw nothing. I'm going crazy wondering about it.'

'Relax,' Garth told him dryly. 'Nobody was anywhere near the building when Collins died.'

Calthorpe shrugged and went out.

Rubbing his chest pensively Garth settled at the desk. 'Whitty, I've seen Mrs.

Collins, had a few words with her. While it's fresh in my mind just jot down these salient points, will you? Er — revolver was first used at bedside in August fifteen years ago, after the Beryl Cleveland affair; Collins used an open car and went to the Darricourt home in it on the night of the murder, afterwards pursuing them half-way to Sussex when his car broke down; and finally Beatrice Collins is not aware of her husband having had anything secret about his person at any time . . . That's all.'

Whittaker whipped the sheet from the typewriter and put it on the blotter. He frowned. 'Sounds to me as if Collins himself murdered that woman, sir. The breakdown business is old fashioned.'

'Beatrice Collins also thinks that her husband murdered Beryl Cleveland, but I don't. The tie up with the car accident is those grass stains I asked you about. Remember?'

'Of course, I remember, but I still don't see the connection.'

'You will in time. It's still only a theory in my mind, and because I don't like being laughed at I'm not trotting it out until I'm positive.'

Whittaker considered the note over the Chief Inspector's shoulder and then scratched his head. ''Didn't have anything secret about him . . . ' Well, why should he?'

Garth sat back in his chair. 'Consider this proposal for a moment: Somebody sent a note to the Yard here for, we now believe, the express purpose of diverting the attention of the police away from the real murder spot. Right?'

'We believe so, sir — yes.'

'All right, then. One point has been bugging me. Why did the killer want to do the job so quietly? Why go to such lengths — dangerous lengths indeed since typewriters can be identified — to make sure of not being seen doing it?'

'Well, it doesn't present much of a problem, sir, does it?' Whittaker gave a bewildered look. 'One hardly wants to be seen doing a murder!'

'I agree — but how many murderers send notes beforehand to divert attention? About one in fifty thousand, I'd say.

You see, Collins could just as easily have been shot at home, shot in his office, shot *anywhere*, without any need of a note beforehand.'

'I suppose so,' Whittaker conceded, frowning. 'What about it, sir?'

'My hunch is that the killer wanted to be sure that Collins could be searched after the killing, without much fear of interruption — and interruption would have been bound to occur in either his home or his office. Sending the note was a clumsy expedient, an effort to divert attention — and dammit, it worked insofar that we at least, and the bobbies in that particular area, were more concentrated round Amberly Building and Terancy Street than anywhere else. The killer did not know that there would be no interruption, but it seemed that every reasonable precaution had been taken to prevent it.'

'Er — yes,' Whittaker said. 'But excuse me for saying it, sir — I haven't the vaguest idea what you're talking about! Why *should* the killer want to search Collins?'

'To get from him — I think — certain signed evidence that could convict him for murder.' Garth looked at Whittaker with subdued amusement in his pale eyes. 'It is more or less established by now that Collins was blackmailing Morton, and had been for fifteen years — ever since the murder date of Beryl Cleveland.'

Whittaker sat down slowly, and nodded ponderously.

'Very well,' Garth said, 'a blackmailer can't possibly extort a thousand quid a month from a man without very reliable evidence of the payer's guilt, can he? A threat to speak the truth wouldn't be strong enough. Even a photograph showing how the murder might have happened, and the person responsible, wouldn't be good enough either. Photographs can be cleverly faked. Yet, says me, Collins must have had something mighty vital in order to squeeze money out of Morton for all those years. Something so damning that Morton didn't dare go to the police and lay a charge of blackmail against Collins. Only one thing seems to suggest itself — something that the

Calligraphy Department could prove is not a fake; something which the tintometer and ultra-violet can show is really fifteen years old; something that can show it has a genuine signature . . . '

'A — a confession!' Whittaker exclaimed.

'Better to say an indictment,' Garth said grimly. 'An indictment from the person who was murdered but who — to be paradoxical — did not die immediately.'

Whittaker was losing the thread again.

'It's now proved beyond cavil that Collins went to see Darricourt on the night of the murder — for business reasons,' Garth went on. 'I'm assuming that that was his reason, that he found Darricourt had left and so followed after him in his car to the Sussex cottage — which address he knew. Then at some point en route he came across the dying body of Beryl Cleveland.'

'How do you know?' Whittaker questioned.

'I don't for certain, but can you tell me how the old girl had grass stains on her clothes without lying in the grass? And if you tell me that she lay in the grass for fun, or before she saw the Darricourts, you're crazy! She was, I believe, strangled by Darricourt — left for dead in the grass somewhere off the road in lonely country. Dead she would undoubtedly have been if Collins had not happened to follow and came across her ... As to how Beryl Cleveland came to be with the Darricourts we don't know — but we'll find out before we're finished.'

'Then?'

Garth brooded. 'Collins, I think, did some fast thinking. The woman was dying. He couldn't save her, but he could use her. I believe he had her write a statement as to who had attacked her, after which she died. He waited until dark, drove back to the Darricourt home, and, knowing only the old and otherwise innocuous housekeeper was present he smuggled the corpse into the house — familiar with the surroundings, of course — and with a piece of cord in exactly the same place as that caused by the strangling, which would show as a weal in the neck, he hung the body in the

293

clothes cupboard. He took a long time removing all traces of his handiwork and got home about three in the morning. Then the case opened, and fell to bits. But Collins was in possession of enough evidence to convict Darricourt, and maybe others, for murder if he did not trip up.'

'Yes, but supposing the thing had been proven as murder on the part of Darricourt? Collins must surely have reckoned on that possibility?'

'Doubtless he did. What he planned to do in that case I don't know — but the fact that he left no clues pointing to Darricourt directly makes it seem that he was fairly sure there wouldn't be enough evidence to convict him. Had it gone otherwise let's make a guess — Collins was head clerk in that firm. I see no reason, had Darricourt been found guilty, why Collins could not have handled things in the firm so neatly that he'd have made himself the boss of it. If that didn't happen — as it didn't — he assured himself with two-fifty pounds a week as long as Darricourt lived and opened up a business on his own account. Certainly he got little out of it because he seems to have lost money as fast as he got it, which immediately blows sky high his supposed genius for foreseeing the market. As to why he set about Darricourt in this fashion — well, we don't know how much hatred or friction there was between the two men.'

'Then,' Whittaker said, 'Darricourt tried to duck the issue by changing his identity?'

'That, I think, was his real reason for it — to dodge Collins. But somehow Collins must have got on to him and kept the sword of Damocles still hanging . . .' Garth crushed his cheroot in the ashtray. 'Obviously Collins must have had good evidence, but he wouldn't keep evidence like that in his home or office where it could be got at. He'd keep it on his person, I think, guarding himself with a gun when he slept. Morton, too, must have been aware of this and knew the only way to get that evidence was to shoot Collins dead, search him in as much safety as possible, and remove the indictment.'

'And you think the killer — Morton, I presume — did get the evidence?'

'I'm as sure as I'm born that he didn't,' Garth answered grimly. 'And neither have we. I can't find a thing among his effects . . . Another point that prompted the murder, I think, was that Collins had raised his demands. Collins told his wife he was bringing off a big deal that would immeasurably improve things for them, and she was fairly sure he meant it. Instead he got shot. The two things tie up.'

Whittaker sighed deeply. 'Far as I can see, sir, it holds together. In fact it has to, inferring as it were from logical premises. But there are still certain points not cleared up. For instance, if Darricourt's wife and maid went with him to Sussex they too must have been in on the strangling. Well, not *must*, but it's very probable.'

'According to the records, only the maid Bella went in the car with Darricourt to the cottage. Mrs. Darricourt went ahead by train.'

'Oh?' Whittaker mused; then, 'There's

another point. Why did Darricourt strangle Beryl Cleveland anyway?'

'Apparently because of the speculations which looked like materialising — to quote Chief Inspector Dawlish. If that had happened Darricourt would have taken a caning. Maybe he thought it better to quietly bump off a wealthy recluse with no relatives or neighbours than to risk bankruptcy. She might even have had some line on him that threatened exposure for his shady manipulations, and there have been plenty of those — even since he has been Morton, but nothing that can be pinned down . . . Maybe lots of things. We've to find out yet.'

'All of which,' Whittaker said, 'proves that Morton is the killer.'

'It makes it look as though it is,' Garth amended. 'There remains the inescapable fact that he never left his office while he was talking to his wife on the telephone and while Collins was murdered.'

'Then what about that maid?' Whittaker demanded. 'We've not included her yet.'

'Who hasn't?' Garth asked cynically.

'I've weighed up that overstuffed domestic from every angle. Just as I've weighed up how Collins died.'

'Then for Pete's sake, how *did* he die?' Whittaker protested.

'All right, I'll tell you. He — '

Garth broke off and glanced up as Albert Knott of the Calligraphy Department knocked on the office door and entered. Whittaker eyed him morosely, conscious of having lost a golden opportunity to lay a ghost in Terancy Street.

'We've got the typewriter you want, Garth,' Knott said, jerking his head vaguely to the open door.

Garth jumped to his feet eagerly. 'That's what I've been waiting for . . . Let's have a look at it.'

He caught the expert's arm and they went along the corridors together to Calligraphy. When they had reached the table where Knott had been making his tests the expert indicated the immense enlargements he had made. Picking up a pencil he pointed to the square-ruled sheet of glass.

'There it is, Garth,' he said. 'All the letters checked with the protractor. See the defect in the 'i' dot? And the 'k' strikes heavily on the right side . . . There are plenty of other identical marks. The machine which typed this is the one you want.'

'Okay! Let me have the original sheet and file the comparison sheet away in readiness for when I want it.'

Knott withdrew the sheet from under the glass graph and handed it across. Upon the bottom was typed — *Machine L/K 46789, Valiant Noiseless Typewriter, Model 5. In possession of the Climax Typewriter Agency, 22 Chandos Street, W.C.*

'See you later,' Garth said, and stalked back through the corridors to his office.

'Any luck, sir?' Whittaker looked up enquiringly.

'All the luck in the world . . . I'm finding out about that typewriter. Get everything recorded and filed ready for action. Before long we'll have this business all tied up with neat bows on it.'

'Yes, sir.' Whittaker sighed and turned

back to his machine, knowing the opportunity had gone — for the time being anyway — for him to discover how Collins had died.

Garth hurried down the corridor outside and to his car. It took him fifteen minutes to find the Climax Typewriter Agency in Chandos Street. It was only a small establishment and filled with steel cabinets, bales of envelopes and paper, rebuilt and new typewriters. A banner advertisement over the counter said VALIANT TYPEWRITERS ARE BEST!

Garth thumped his fist down on a bell knob and in response a short, round-faced man emerged from somewhere in the back regions.

'Yessir?' He came to the counter.

'Scotland Yard,' Garth said, and showed his warrant card. He tugged the specimen sheet from his pocket. 'Which machine does this belong to?'

'Now let me see . . . ' The man repeated the registration number and then swung round to survey his stock. 'I seem to remember — ah, yes!' He raised a finger dramatically. 'This is it, sir.'

He came waddling round the counter and indicated a machine standing by itself on a small table. It was brand new and apparently an excellent piece of workmanship. Garth stooped, checked the manufacturer's number, and then nodded.

'Good enough. Let me have a list of all the people who've hired this out recently, will you?'

The proprietor shrugged and looked vague. 'I'm sorry, Inspector, but nobody ever hired this out. I don't allow it. No man in his right senses would hire out a brand new machine. Only the rebuilt ones . . . No, sir! This is for sale only.'

Garth was silent; he had not expected this. Yet it was logical. Hiring out a brand new machine would certainly be asking for it.

'I've reason to believe,' he said quietly, 'that somebody or other used this machine recently, and for a very important purpose. Surely you can help me in some way?'

'I don't quite see how I can, sir. This machine only came in a fortnight ago, and being the best in the bunch I put it there as a specimen to catch the eye. The only person to touch it was that man you sent from Scotland Yard, and myself, of course.'

'Mmmm — quite.' Garth turned and looked at the door, at the narrow pavement where people were passing and glancing in casually. A thought stirred in his mind.

'Tell me something . . . Has anybody been in here recently and asked for something that necessitated you leaving the shop at all? Or going into those back regions of yours?' Garth peered towards a doorway dimly visible at the back of the shop, through which the proprietor had originally emerged.

'Basement, Inspector. I keep my stock down there.'

'I see. Well, did anybody make it necessary for you to go down there?'

'I get lots of people in here. I really can't remember.'

Garth eyed him coldly. 'Don't be too hasty about it, sir. This is very important — and we need co-operation. I'm in no hurry. Just think it out.'

The proprietor was duly chastened. 'Depends how long ago it was.'

'Oh, say within the last fortnight.' Garth glanced towards the door. 'While you think it out I'll just take a look at your shop window.'

He went outside and on to the pavement. It was not the shop window that interested him, but the narrow oblong of glass window set level with the pavement. Through it he gazed into a basement, electric-lighted, and filled with equipment and stores. Smiling tautly to himself he came back into the shop.

'I can think of one woman,' the proprietor said, glancing up. 'She asked me for a box of rather unusual-sized envelopes. I showed her all I had in here but she wasn't satisfied, so I went below to see what I could find.'

Garth's death mask settled slowly into place. 'How long were you in the basement, sir?'

'About five minutes. But I found the size she wanted.'

'I see. What did she look like, this customer?'

'I've a vague idea she was heavily built and looked rather pasty-faced. Fairly tall, too. Middle-aged, I'd say.'

Garth looked at the typewriter reflectively, then: 'I'd like to borrow this machine for a couple of hours, sir. We'll go over it for fingerprints and return it in good order. Here's a receipt for it.'

The proprietor took the signed slip when Garth had finished scribbling it out.

'Quite all right to me, Inspector, if it helps you. Shall I give you a hand to — '

'No.' Garth waved him away quickly. 'Don't touch it; I'll handle it.'

He eased his hand under its base and raised it. He carried it outside, and laid it carefully on the floor in the back of the car. Then he drove back swiftly to the Yard, where he finally set it down on a table in the Fingerprints Department.

Arthur Carson, in charge, came over and looked at it. 'Now what?' he enquired.

'I want you to go over it for prints,' Garth said, flexing his fingers after his effort in carrying the machine. 'Two lots I know you'll find — or should. Those of Calthorpe and the proprietor of the typewriter store. But I'm hoping there may be others. Dig out everything you can, file them and photograph them. Should be something on that roller knob, at least. Anyhow, keep me advised.'

'Okay. We'll get on with it right away.'

19

When he reached the office the Chief Inspector poked his head inside.

'Anything happened, Whitty?'

Sergeant Whittaker turned to look at him. 'No, sir, nothing fresh. How about the typewriter? Did you find out about it?'

'It's being worked over by Dabs. Tell you about it later. I'm on my way to Mrs. Morton's before the afternoon gets too old.'

He departed again and returned to his car. Grim-faced and thoughtful he drove out to Kensington and arrived at the Morton home in twenty minutes. It was Bella who opened the door.

'Good afternoon, Inspector,' she greeted, in her deep, slow voice. 'You wish to see the mistress, I suppose?'

'I do,' Garth acknowledged, and stepped inside as she motioned him into the hall. Hat in hand he watched her powerful figure go across to the drawing room. Then Mrs. Morton appeared, dressed to perfection, that infectious smile on her face and her hand extended. Stolidly, Bella went off towards the kitchen regions.

'Well, well, my dear Inspector, I am so glad you decided to call again . . . ' Hazel Morton shook his hand vigorously. 'Come along in and tell me the news. I've told Bella to bring in some tea.'

Garth muttered something inwardly and forced a smile. He followed Hazel Morton's smoothly rounded figure into the drawing room and finally sat down on the edge of an armchair as she motioned to it. With that innate grace she possessed she settled on the divan opposite him.

'Now, Mr. Garth, what has been happening?' she enquired earnestly. 'I think' — her blue eyes regarded him roguishly — 'you're one of the most interesting men I've ever met. You don't mind me saying that?'

'Not at all, madam, if it pleases you.' Garth compressed his lips. 'I just dropped in to ask a few more questions.'

'By all means.' She spread delicate hands invitingly.

'Good. Tell me then — did you know your husband's first wife?'

'His first wife? Oh, you mean Ruby? Yes, I knew Ruby very well indeed.'

'Did you, though?' Garth said, watching her intently. 'I feel compelled to point out, madam, that you didn't mention her name when I asked you if your name was Ruby.'

'But was there any necessity?' She looked surprised and then contrite. 'I'm so sorry if I've transgressed, but after all you only asked me if my name was Ruby, and I said it wasn't and that I do not like the name. I certainly didn't think at that moment of Ruby Morton. Why should I? She's been dead fifteen years or so.'

Garth realized he was once again fighting that sense of smothering. The more he tried to twist things round and unsettle her the more she smiled and slid out with easy, charming grace.

He was pondering on his next lead when Bella entered with the inevitable tea wagon. Same again — tea, cream cakes, buns.

'That will be all, Bella,' Hazel Morton told her, and looked under her long lashes at Garth. 'I know what you like, Inspector — sugar and not too much milk.'

'Thank you, madam,' he said gruffly, taking the cup from her. 'And no cake, thank you. My dyspepsia, you know.'

She nodded sympathetically. 'I'm sure you ought to try magnesia, Inspector . . . You won't think me too awful if I try an éclair?'

'Not at all.' Garth stirred his tea with unmeaning vigour. 'Now, madam,' he said firmly, 'I've quite a few things to ask you. A moment or two ago you referred to Ruby Morton. She wasn't Morton then: her surname was Darricourt. Legally you are also Hazel Darricourt. Your husband changed his name but not legitimately.'

She was looking eagerly amongst the crockery, the grey streaks in her dark hair very obvious for a moment.

'Where did I put that spoon now — ? Ah!' She whipped it up and smiled. 'Yes,' she added lightly, sitting back and performing her amazing balancing act with tea and cake simultaneously, 'I know my husband changed his name.'

'Oh . . . ' Garth felt a rather deadening sensation, and it was not indigestion either. 'You know? You told me that you had never heard the name of Darricourt.'

'Did I? But how silly of me! I must have forgotten for the moment. After all, fifteen years is a strain on the memory, don't you think? Matter of fact I asked Dudley to change his name, but I didn't know it had to be done legally to make it stick. Anyway, I'm not bothered very much about it. What's in a name? You know the old saying.'

'Why did you ask him to do that?' Garth demanded.

'Well, to tell you the truth . . . ' She looked at him intently and glanced about as if to make sure nobody else were present. 'There was a bit of awful scandal! You've no idea! It even involved murder!'

Garth gave a brief smile and took another mouthful from the teacup. 'I know about that, and if you are also

310

referring to the murder of Beryl Cleveland in the clothes cupboard of your husband's home in Hampstead — as it was at that time — that is no secret either. Not to me.'

'Oh!' She looked vague for a moment, then with a slight jerk of her shoulders she bit a piece out of the éclair. 'Well, then, that saves me an awful lot of explanation. I needn't have pretended I didn't know the name of Darricourt, need I?' She looked shyly at him through her lashes. 'And a little time before that there was something unsavoury about embezzling too. It was because of these things that I asked Dudley to change his name and start all over again. The police couldn't prove anything of course, but that isn't always sufficient, is it? I mean, when a thing is neither proven nor disproved a sort of horrible stigma remains. I wasn't going to marry Dudley with that hanging over him.'

'Mmmm — I see. I gather you had known Mr. Morton some time before the death of his wife?'

'Ye-es, quite some time,' she admitted.

311

'To be frank, Ruby and Dudley were not at all happy together. One of those incompatible marriages, you know. I do believe the poor dear was suing for divorce, or something, then pneumonia overtook her and it wasn't necessary.'

'Uh-huh,' Garth acknowledged, picking up his teacup again. 'As I understand it, madam, harking back to the night of the murder, Mr. Morton followed on to the Sussex cottage after his wife had gone. He went over by car with the maid Bella, didn't he?'

'I believe so, yes.' It was not absolutely definite but it did seem to Garth that Hazel Morton was not eating the éclair with quite the same nonchalance. It even looked as though she might be thinking hard, and deeply . . .

'I think it is so, madam. We have those facts in our records. How did it happen, do you know, that Bella did not go with Mrs. Darricourt?'

'I'm sure I don't know, inspector. How could I? I wasn't married to Dudley then, and I had only passing knowledge of his movements. I'm afraid I can't tell you anything about it.'

Garth reflected, then he took out his propelling silver pencil and made a few notes, set the pencil down in the chair beside him and considered what he had written. When he looked up again he beheld Hazel Morton's eyes upon him in puzzled interest.

'Oh, forgive me, madam!' He smiled suddenly and put the paper away in his pocket. 'Just a note or two I don't want to forget. I wonder if you would mind if I had a word with — '

He was going to say 'the maid,' then a sudden change of thought was upon him. If what he believed were true he might only come up against more evasions, one helping out the other. There was a better way round it than that.

'Er — never mind.' Garth cleared his throat and put his teacup on the wagon. 'Am I right in thinking, Mrs. Morton, that your life has been happy these past fifteen years, since you married Mr. Morton?'

It seemed, on the face of it, a surprising switch in topic. It was genial conversation, divested of the dark cloak of suspicion and murder.

'Ideally,' she answered, and then she drained her own teacup and set it down. 'Just as I thought at first, if Dudley and I could only marry we'd make a grand thing of our lives.' She reflected, then: 'Ruby was never the right woman for him, you know. She was content with the little things, had no ambition, no wish at all to see her husband a financial power in the land. I feel some slight pride in the fact that his present eminence has been in no small measure due to my encouragement. I've always helped him upwards — advanced him.'

'And yourself, madam?' Garth murmured dryly, sitting back.

She regarded him in surprise. 'I? Of course, Inspector. I am not the stay-in-four-walls type of woman, believe me. I wanted him to succeed so that I too could rise in the world. I always wanted to know what it was like to be influential, ever since being a little girl.'

Garth was looking was looking vaguely conciliatory. 'You are, I feel, one of those women who have been taught a great deal

314

from early life? Parents in, shall I say, a somewhat menial position?'

'Oh, my father was a gunsmith. Nothing there I could do, though I used to help him a little until I was about fifteen. He had a good trade, far as it went. I wanted something better. Naturally, when the chance came for me to advance myself by marrying Dudley I took it with both hands. I wouldn't allow the stigma of that horrible embezzlement and later that murder business to cloud his chances, and that is why I asked him to completely change his identity.'

'When exactly did you meet him, Mrs. Morton? Where?'

She shrugged. 'In London. I think it started in a café when I dropped my handbag.'

Garth could feel himself slipping and smothering again. He got to his feet and thumped gently at his chest.

'Well, madam, this has been most interesting,' he said as she rose too. 'I find you most helpful each time I call.'

'I enjoy having you here, you know. You're so different from the ordinary run of men, even from my husband's everlasting stockbroking, which sometimes gets on my nerves. There is something fascinating about crime, don't you think?'

'Perhaps,' Garth answered, then he glanced at his watch. 'I've taken up enough of your time Mrs. Morton. Thank you for the tea.'

She saw him to the door, smiling and waving at him as he went down the front path to his car. His face impassive, Garth drove back to Scotland Yard, and it was close on five as he re-entered the office.

Grimly thoughtful, he went over to his desk. Whittaker, sensing the aura was unsafe to disturb, motioned to the blotter where a fingerprints report and a telephone message were lying.

'They came during the afternoon, sir.'

Garth looked at them absently. The telephone report indicated that the gun was a 38 revolver — Z.427866, and manufactured by Webley and Scott. It had been purchased on January 7, twelve years earlier, from Medway and Wilkinson, Gaming and General Gunsmiths,

Tottenham Court Road. The name given was John Elswick.

'Alias Vincent Darricourt alias Dudley Morton,' Garth said tossing the report down. 'Which doesn't help much . . . '

He picked up the one from Fingerprints and read it through.

Fingerprints report on Valiant Typewriter submitted: Two or three sets of fingerprints are visible on keys and roller knobs. Photographed and submitted herewith. Prints are Exceptional Arch, Twinned Loop, and Whorl.

Garth looked at them in enlargement and numbered 1, 2, and 3. He smiled to himself.

'If the typewriter's done with, sir, Dabs wants to know if it should be sent back to the dealer,' Whittaker remarked.

Garth nodded. 'Yes, do that. I've squeezed all I want out of it. Take this report back to Dabs and tell 'em to see if any of the prints check with Vincent Darricourt in M.O. If not, I'll probably find a set to check later on.'

'Right, sir.' Whittaker half moved to the door, then he turned back. 'Sir, I'm finding it hard to keep my interest suppressed. Has anything happened?'

'Sort of,' Garth admitted, brooding. 'But don't ask me to tell you anything because I'm still not sure — that alibi has to be cracked before we can see what we're getting at.'

'It's more or less sure, though, that Morton is our man, isn't it?'

'Nothing's sure, Whitty — and that probably least of all.'

'Least of all! But surely, sir, if — '

'Don't bother me now!' Garth jammed a cheroot between his teeth and glared. 'I want to think. I've a knotty problem to work out . . .'

Whittaker fell silent. He picked up the fingerprint report and went out, leaving Garth slumped in his swivel chair with his eyes on the blotter.

'Twenty years,' he muttered. 'She did say twenty years. No reason to doubt that. I wonder if — there has to be a connection somewhere!'

He rubbed the sides of his face irritably. Then presently he brightened somewhat and picked up the telephone.

20

When Sergeant Whittaker came back into the office he found Garth's mood of sour impatience had vanished.

'Dabs report that Vincent Darricourt's prints don't check with any of those on the typewriter,' Whittaker said.

'Okay. I'm not worried.'

Whittaker shrugged and went towards his typewriter to study the next batch of shorthand notes for transcription. Garth pulled open the drawer of his desk and dumped the effects of Collins on the blotter — the wallet, containing the report of the blackmail acquittal, the money, and the bunch of keys. One by one he examined each article minutely, switching on the desk light to see them better — but at the end of ten minutes he shook his head.

'Hanged if I know where he kept that confession,' he muttered. 'Wonder if anything was sewn in his clothes? Think

I'll step over and have a look.'

As he got to his feet there was a knock and Calthorpe came in. There was upon his calmly impudent face that suppressed expression that usually meant he had something good to impart.

'I'll see about those clothes later,' Garth added, as Whittaker glanced at him. 'Okay, Calthorpe, what have you got?'

'Dudley Morton is on his last legs, sir. I've checked on it through the banks and Stock Exchange with Mason and Pascal helping me. It all adds up to the same thing.'

'Last legs? You mean bankruptcy?'

'Exactly, sir. Far as I can make out he's been playing tick with the law of the land for a good many years . . . '

'You're telling me,' Garth growled. 'He once got five years penal anyway . . . Well, go on.'

'As far as I can make out certain honest firms have got their heads together to crush him. He's about on the brink and stands to lose everything he's got. I'm no stockbroker, but it has something to do with cornering.' Calthorpe shrugged. 'Financially, it appears that Morton has about three months to live unless he pulls together everything he's got and makes some sort of spectacular swindling comeback.'

'Unless he pulls together everything he's got,' Garth repeated slowly, rubbing his hands. 'You've put it very neatly, Calthorpe . . . All right, that's all — and thanks.'

Garth chuckled softly to himself as Calthorpe went out. 'This simplifies things enormously, as well as verifying my innermost thoughts. Now let me see . . . ' He felt for his pencil impatiently, then paused and seemed to remember something. Reaching for the telephone he yanked it up.

'Hello — get me the home of Dudley Morton, please, and ask for Mrs. Morton.' He waited, humming gently to himself, then at that familiar voice in the receiver he gave an apologetic laugh. 'Oh, Mrs. Morton! Sorry to bother you again, but I believe I've left my propelling pencil over at your place — '

The receiver chattered and Garth compressed his lips through an interval, slanting an eye at the faintly grinning Whittaker.

'Yes, yes,' Garth agreed. 'I must have left it in the armchair when I made that note while talking to you. I wonder if you'd mind sending the maid over with it? It's the sentimental value — yes. Thanks so much. Pardon? Oh, yes, I'll be here for some time yet.' He rang off, took out a handkerchief and mopped his face.

'Whew, can that woman talk! I don't wonder Morton's bankrupt after fifteen years with her. The wonder is he isn't going crazy. Hmmm — well, so far, so good.' He looked round the office tolerantly.

'Unlike you to forget something, sir,' Whittaker commented.

Garth's grin faded. 'It was that woman, Whitty: she gets you so wound up you don't know what you are doing. By the way, I'm going to ask this maid a few questions when she gets here. You might let me know what you think of her answers.'

'Glad to, sir, even though I have missed out parts in between. Last definite bit of news I had in this business was about the presumed indictment on the part of Collins. I've got no further. Don't even know how far you've got with the typewriter, nor do I know how Collins really died.'

'Proof, my boy, proof!' Garth admonished him. 'I have to be sure of that first. I've got practically all of it now.' He rubbed his jaw. 'I hope to have everything ready by the inquest tomorrow.'

He glanced again at Collins's effects on the desk.

'Wish I knew where this outsized key fits . . . ' Then with a shrug he swept the stuff into the desk drawer and locked it.

'You'll want me to take this maid's statement down, sir?'

'You'd better, yes, even though I'm having it recorded as well.' Garth looked about his desk and picked up a manilla folder, glanced at the unimportant papers inside it, and finally placed it at the opposite corner on the other side of the desk. 'Come into my parlour,' he murmured.

At length there was a knock on the office door and a constable ushered in Bella.

Garth eyed her, pressed the button under the desk edge. The woman studied him with her impassive grey eyes as she came forward, ponderously deliberate, to the desk. She was dressed in a brown tweed coat, by no means new, and a black straw hat that she wore rather far back on her head.

'It's your pencil, Inspector,' she said. 'It had lodged in the side of the armchair. Here it is.'

He nodded amiably and took it as she handed it across. 'Sit down, Bella, won't you? Sorry to have to give you such a trip but there was nobody I could spare from here to come and get it.'

She settled in the chair he indicated on the opposite side of the desk, not a trace of expression on her pasty face.

'While you are here,' Garth resumed, 'there's a question I'd like to ask you. You don't have to answer it, but I'd be glad if you would . . . What is your surname?'

She appeared unperturbed. 'Gibson, sir. Might I ask why you want to know?'

Garth smiled disarmingly. 'In writing up the records in this case I have to give every detail of the people connected with it. Naturally I can't just put down your Christian name and let it go at that. Bella Gibson, eh? I'd better put that down in the file right away — ' He glanced across the desk. 'Oh, there it is! Would you mind?'

The maid picked it up from in front of her and handed it across. Garth nodded his thanks, opened it, and then wrote something she couldn't see at the bottom of a sheet of paper.

'Well, that's that!' Garth set the folder on one side. 'Now, was there anything else I was going to ask you? Save me running out to Kensington again — oh, yes, I know! You would of course know Mr. Morton's former wife, Ruby?'

'Yes, sir, I knew her. I worked for her, of course, before Mr. Morton married the present mistress.'

'You also know all about the change of name and identity from Darricourt to Morton?' Garth asked. She nodded composedly.

'I know most of the things that have

happened in that family, sir. In twenty years, so to speak, one gets on the inside of things.'

'Yes, I suppose so.' There was a touch of grimness in Garth's voice. 'Fifteen years ago, Bella, on the night Beryl Cleveland was hanged, you went to Sussex with your master in his car, did you not? Following on to the cottage where his first wife had already gone?'

'I did, yes. I suppose the mistress told you that?'

'No,' Garth said quietly, 'she didn't. She said she had not the least idea what you did. She hardly could have, since she wasn't present.'

A slight change of expression came to the blunt features — but it did not develop into anything.

'Well, anyway, I went there,' Bella said stolidly. 'Is that what you want to know, sir?'

'That,' Garth replied, 'is *all* I want to know. And thanks for the pencil, Bella. Good evening.'

After she left the office, Garth glanced at Whittaker. 'Well, Whitty, what reactions?'

'Negative, sir. I don't know what led up to this. She seems like a solid, worthy domestic, well dug in with the Mortons after twenty years of service — '

'Exactly — well dug in!' Garth wagged a finger at him. 'And you'll be tremendously dug in for information, too, in a while if what I suspect is correct.'

He got to his feet and picked up the file the woman had handed him.

'I'm taking this over to Dabs for a quick check-up, and having a word with Pierce in the radio department. I'll be back pretty soon.'

He strode out energetically and left Whittaker alone with his speculations. There was before Whittaker a positive wilderness of unexplained things. Finally he went over to the piled notes and records on his superior's desk and went through them briefly. Some of Garth's scribbles were unreadable, and those he could read, being plain statements of fact, gave nothing away.

He had spent quite half an hour in this fashion when the door reopened and Garth returned. He was looking genial again, a satisfied grin on his emaciated face. With a gesture he threw down the manilla file.

'Proof, my boy,' he said calmly. 'Now I can tell you; Bella Gibson typed the note which had all of us staring cow-eyed at that building in Terancy Street, and which lured the police away from the murder spot. I guessed as much when Mrs. Morton told me amidst her usual gushings that Bella did quite a deal of secretarial work for Morton at home. If that didn't include typing I decided I must be crazy.'

Garth began to prowl round the office.

'The thing was to make sure, naturally. You know yourself how we had the typewriter tracked down and checked. The fingerprints on it belong to three people — possibly the typewriter store proprietor, to Calthorpe when he tested it, and to Bella Gibson. I took the risk that she wasn't wearing gloves, which she could hardly be to type.'

'Funny the prints aren't all on top of each other on the keys,' Whittaker mused.

'The keys themselves are hopeless for

prints. It's the roller knob that gives it away. It is, according to mathematicians, a two million to one chance that three people grasping a typewriter roller knob to turn it would alight on exactly the same place as the preceding person. And since the machine is new, used as an exhibition piece by the proprietor, no more than three prints were likely to be on it. When I called on this proprietor he described a person who exactly fits the description of the Gibson girl.'

'I see. But how did she do it? Hire out the machine?'

'No.' Garth's jaw set hard. 'A typewriter was needed to type a note which would distract attention. How to get one without anybody knowing about it? The typewriter in question was clearly visible from the pavement through the glass door of the shop. On its carrier it says — 'Valiant *Noiseless*.' Now, we have to assume that Bella prowled until she found the right place for her little plot. The typewriter store has a basement and the stores therein are visible from outside through a window . . .

'So Bella went in the shop, asked for something that made it necessary for the proprietor to have to go prowling through his basement. In those few minutes Bella typed out the warning and envelope on the Valiant Noiseless. Being a good typist she'd do it in roughly three minutes. It was a risk, but what a delightful way of using an unknown machine which, she thought, could never be traced.'

'And the paper?' Whittaker questioned. 'Don't forget she used paper identical to that recently bought by Morton's firm.'

'I've thought that one out. To go and buy different paper would perhaps have drawn attention much more conspicuously than to use a well-known brand used by a business house like Morton's. So she used that — making it so obvious that she thought by that very fact to prevent it seeming suspicious.'

'Very neat,' Whittaker admitted. 'But amateur! She should have known that typing can always be traced.'

'Outside of those who study crime detection very few do know it,' Garth answered. 'She probably thought, if she considered the matter at all, that a new typewriter can't be traced. But that also is a fallacy — heaven be praised!'

'Then you didn't really forget your pencil at all? You did it on purpose to get her here? To make her confess — or at any rate admit certain things.'

'I didn't even refer to the typewriter, and you know it. I'm not saying anything until I'm ready to spring the trap. I admit the pencil, though; but I didn't ask her here to extract a confession . . . '

Whittaker stirred. 'Look, sir, this means we've been up the wrong tree! *She* killed Collins — but don't ask me how! Being only a maid-cum-secretary Morton would surely never put her up to it, even if she had been in the family for twenty years.'

Garth pulled out a cheroot and lighted it absently.

'A little while ago, Whitty, I rang up the government department holding employment records,' he said. 'I asked them to trace back fifteen years and find out whom Beryl Cleveland had employed as maid . . . You can guess the answer to that one, eh?'

'Bella Gibson?'

'Exactly! She was employed by Beryl Cleveland until a few years before Beryl Cleveland was murdered.'

★ ★ ★ ★

Sergeant Whittaker left Scotland Yard at seven-thirty with Garth still at his desk, waiting for a call from the Radio Department — and he did not see him again until in the office the following morning. He arrived at ten o'clock as usual, his hollow-cheeked face set in hard lines. He was carrying an attaché case, which from the bump it made when he dumped it on the desk it seemed to contain something pretty heavy.

'Books,' he explained briefly, seeing Whittaker's glance. 'They can be the hell of a help when you want to bolster up a theory. There's an inquest this afternoon, Whitty, so I'd better polish off the unfinished business this morning. Get me through to the Morton house, will you?'

Whittaker nodded and Garth turned his attention to the neatly filed dossier of information on the Granville Collins case which — acting as secretary — Whittaker had placed on the desk for his inspection.

He leafed through the pages until Whittaker got the number, then took hold of the instrument and sat back in his chair.

'Hello, Mrs. Morton?' Garth grinned at something as he listened to her. 'Yes. Yes, indeed. Well, I'll tell you — I've run into a problem here which only one person can solve — and that's you. 'Phones are not the most private instrument sometimes and I can't get over to you. Could you come along to my office?'

Again the chattering and Garth listened in bored patience.

'All right,' he said finally. 'In about half an hour — right.'

He put the instrument down and looked up. 'One thing more from her, Whitty, and I have all I need.'

'What,' Whittaker asked, 'is the one thing?'

'I want to find out how Collins usually dressed.'

'But we *know* how he dressed, don't we?'

'On the morning of his death, yes. We don't know any more than that, and it's vital that we should. You'll probably grasp why later on.'

Whittaker frowned. He was clearly still baffled.

'I had a look through Collins's clothes again last night,' Garth resumed. 'There is no sign there of the confession — or rather indictment — which I am sure ought to exist, and hasn't been taken from him. So where the devil *is* it?'

'Might be sewn up in his wallet,' Whittaker suggested.

'It isn't. I made sure of that.' Garth unlocked the desk drawer irritably and pulled out the objects again. Whittaker stood looking over his shoulder.

'Something occurs to me, sir,' he said slowly. That key ring: one key unlocked the office safe, another the desk drawers and so on — but we didn't account for that big key.'

'And he always chained his keys to the mattress at night and nearly went crazy one time when they were lost.' Garth narrowed his eyes and took the bunch of keys to the window. Using a pocket lens he peered at the outsize key.

'Whitty, my bright lad, I do believe you've got it!' he exclaimed. 'You can't see it with the naked eye, but under this lens there is a tiny ridge of solidified metal visible round the end of this key shaft. As though it has been sawn off and then re-welded! I'm taking it along to the lab and get the boys to take it apart. A sealed key stem is a first-class place to hide a note!'

He turned and hurried out of the office, and when at length he came back he found that Mrs. Morton had arrived. She was dressed in a fashionable two-piece, and seated at one side of the desk.

'Good morning, Inspector! So this is where you think up your problems, is it?' She looked about her in demure interest.

'And solve them, madam, as a rule,' he answered gravely, and settled in his swivel chair. 'I'm sorry to have to drag you over here like this, but — '

'Oh, I don't mind, Inspector!' Her bright blue eyes were studying him with a touch of roguishness.

'Now, madam . . . You say that you knew Granville Collins very well indeed. I wonder if you could tell me how he dressed?'

She looked momentarily shocked. 'Really, Inspector!'

'Don't misunderstand,' Garth said heavily. 'I'm checking back on some information I have. Did Collins dress well, or badly? Would you say that he was a dandy?'

'Er — no, I wouldn't say that he was, nor was he a sloven.' She smiled. 'I'd describe him as the well dressed man about town. The city man, you know. They have a distinctive look — striped trousers, and such like.'

'Mmmm . . . ' Garth tightened his lips and considered something in the Collins dossier. 'I have it here that he was, as a rule, a badly dressed man — '

'No!' Hazel Morton declared firmly. 'To the best of my knowledge he was usually dressed in black coat and vest with striped trousers, bowler hat, a white handkerchief in his breast pocket.'

Garth gave a nod and closed the dossier up again. 'Somebody must have been leading me up the garden path.'

Whittaker, taking down the statement, frowned. Nobody had ever said what Collins's attire had been. Mrs. Collins had said that he — Whittaker caught himself on the edge of an astonishing fact and glanced up sharply. He met Garth's eyes as the Chief Inspector got to his feet.

'Will you pardon me a moment, madam?' he asked, smiling. 'I have something I must do. Be back in a second or so.'

He went out and Whittaker found himself under scrutiny from those bright blue eyes. Yes, as Garth had intimated, Hazel Morton had probably been a very attractive woman when twenty years younger.

'What do you do, Sergeant?' she enquired naively.

'As the C.I. tells me chiefly, madam. He finds the evidence and I gather it all together in a dossier.'

'Then you'll know all about this awful business concerning Mr. Collins, then?

Including who did it?'

Whittaker did not say anything. He was too well trained. He breathed out an unheard sigh of relief as Garth re-entered the office, rubbing his hands. Whittaker knew that sign and waited interestedly.

Garth sat down at his desk again and beamed. 'Now where were we — ? Oh, yes, Collins's mode of dress. Well, I think I could do with a bit more information on that even yet. I wonder if your husband could spare time to get over here for a moment?'

The woman looked surprised but passed no comment. Garth picked up the telephone. He growled out his order, then presently —

'Garth here, Mr. Morton. I've got some interesting news for you. I'd be glad if you could hop over to the office for a moment. Your wife is here, by the way — eh? Yes, your wife. In five minutes? Right.'

Garth put the telephone down and turned to his scratchpad, wrote swiftly and tore the sheet off. He motioned Whittaker and handed it to him. His face remained impassive in spite of the words on the paper —

Have Calthorpe and Mason pick up Bella Gibson and bring her here. Return here as quickly as you can.

Hazel Morton sighed. 'Does it matter what he was dressed in? Or is it what you detectives would call an important clue?'

'It depends on the circumstances,' Garth replied ambiguously.

'Oh, really?' She looked faintly troubled. 'Whom do you think murdered him, Mr. Garth? Or don't you know yet?'

He smiled. 'I've known for some little time. But it was just something of a task fitting things together. When a man is found dead in an office, shot, and with nobody ever having been near him in that office, it's a knotty problem. That has now been overcome.'

She nodded slowly and looked at her gloves. Garth contemplated the dossier for the second time. Whittaker returned presently and gave an almost imperceptible nod; then before he could sit at his desk there was a knock on the door and he opened it to admit Dudley Morton.

''Morning, Inspector,' he greeted briefly, putting down his hat — then he glanced at his wife. 'Hello, Hazel — what brought you here?'

'The Inspector wanted to check on the way Gran used to dress.'

Morton looked at Garth sharply. 'What concern is that of my wife's, Inspector?'

Garth sat imperturbably and motioned Whittaker. 'Give Mr. Morton a seat, Sergeant.'

The broker ignored the cigarette box Garth pushed towards him and instead aimed a sharp, suspicious glance across the desk. 'What do you want to know, Inspector?'

'I want to know what you meant by having your maid type a document on a typewriter owned by the Climax Typewriter Agency, and then having it mailed to the Assistant Commissioner — said document warning us that Granville Collins would die in his office between nine and nine-thirty.'

Morton changed his mind. He reached for a cigarette and lighted it carefully. 'It's no concern of mine what the maid does,' he replied briefly. 'Nor is it any concern of hers what I do. You should know that.'

'Should I?' Garth regarded him with snakelike calm. 'She used paper from your office supply and she used a machine which has since been identified. I also know that she is an expert typist . . . ' Garth's eyes moved to the woman. 'You see, Mrs. Morton, you mentioned that Bella did a lot of secretarial work at home for your husband.'

Morton and his wife exchanged glances. The woman gave a shrug.

'Pretty nearly twenty years ago,' Garth went on deliberately, 'Bella Gibson was employed by Beryl Cleveland, a wealthy recluse who was murdered five years or so after Bella had left her employ. I don't know what sort of an employer Beryl Cleveland was, but I believe that Bella had no objections to seeing her murdered.'

'Really, Inspector, this is preposterous!' Morton protested.

'I further believe,' Garth went on stolidly, 'that she was with you when

Beryl Cleveland was murdered. You went to your Sussex cottage after your first wife had gone ahead there by train, Mr. Morton, and took Bella with you. That is beyond dispute. You went in your car.'

'What about it?' Morton snapped.

'Beryl Cleveland,' Garth said, 'was murdered on the route to the cottage — out in the open country. She was then laid, or else thrown, on the grass, probably at the side of the road. Even a dry ditch was used, maybe. Bella Gibson was a witness to the occurrence . . . and so were you, Mrs. Morton.'

'But I wasn't there!' she protested, giving the desktop a thump. 'What — what sort of a tissue is this?'

'Listen to me, madam. It has been proven as near as can be that Beryl Cleveland was strangled and thrown in grass: grass stains on her clothes prove that. It is also proven that Granville Collins went in search of you, Mr. Morton, over a business deal. You had then left your home, on the way to the cottage. Collins followed you, in his open car, and found the body of Beryl

Cleveland. Perhaps he saw it, perhaps he heard groans; I don't know. But I do know that he found her. She told him who had attacked her — and that indictment includes three people. You, Mr. Morton, you, Mrs. Morton, and Bella.'

'I've had about enough of this!' Morton glared. 'There's no proof — nothing!'

'No?' Garth slanted his colourless eyes at Hazel Morton. 'Last evening when I had a few words with Bella I asked her this question — ' He opened the dossier and read: ' "Fifteen years ago, Bella, on the night Beryl Cleveland was hanged, you went with your master to Sussex in the car, didn't you?' She answered — 'I did, yes. I suppose the *mistress* told you that?' Now, you, Mrs. Morton, had told me that you hadn't the least idea of the movements of Mr. Morton on that night. Only one thing could have prompted Bella to her quite natural observation — namely, that you were present! She had forgotten after such a lapse of time that you were not supposed to be there.'

'That still doesn't prove anything,'

Morton commented sourly.

'I think it does,' Garth answered. 'I'll go further and gamble that you, Mrs. Morton, were the prime mover in wanting Beryl Cleveland out of the way.'

'Why should I?' she asked curtly, all her vapouring extinguished.

'Because you were going to marry Morton — divorce proceedings being already in progress — and you knew that if certain speculations of Beryl Cleveland's matured, your intended husband would be penniless, which thought you couldn't bear. You said yourself that you wanted, even as a girl, to climb high socially. The only way to stop anything coming to Beryl Cleveland was to kill her. And you were reasonably sure you wouldn't be involved because at that time you were not definitely, in the legal sense that is, connected with Mr. Morton.'

Morton knocked ash savagely from his cigarette to the floor and his wife sat gazing before her fixedly.

'Somehow,' Garth went on, 'Beryl Cleveland was lured into meeting you that night. I believe it was either the work of Bella, her ex-maid — or it was your work, Mrs. Morton. As a woman of undoubted charm of manner you could easily get her to meet your husband . . . and her death.'

'You haven't a scrap of real evidence,' Morton breathed. 'You can't prove any of this — ever! And I'll make you smart for it, too!'

Garth smiled frozenly, then glanced up as Whittaker opened the door. Bella Gibson came in, Calthorpe holding her elbow.

'All right,' Garth said briefly. 'That's all, Calthorpe. Take a seat, Miss Gibson.'

The maid looked surprised and then settled quietly in the hide armchair by the doorway.

'I was just remarking, Miss Gibson, that you went with Mr. Morton to Sussex on that night fifteen years ago, didn't you?'

'Yes, sir. I told you that yesterday evening.'

'And you were originally employed by Beryl Cleveland some years before she met her death, were you not?'

'Er — ' Bella Gibson wilted under the icy coldness in the Chief Inspector's eyes. 'Yes,' she admitted.

'And you had no liking for Beryl Cleveland, had you?'

Sullenness came to the woman's heavy face. 'I don't see why I should answer that.'

'You don't have to,' Garth replied. 'I know you hadn't. You even thought it would be a good idea if she were murdered, and that is why you helped Mr. Morton — Darricourt as he was then — to do it.'

'What!' The maid had jumped to her feet in sudden anger. She swung round on her employer. 'Mr. Morton! You promised me that you'd protect me — '

'Sit down, woman!' Morton breathed harshly. 'Sit down!'

'Thanks,' Garth said, as the maid obeyed. 'You know, Miss Gibson, you'd save yourself an awful lot of grief if you'd admit the truth. We know all about what you did, but the more lies you tell the worse it will be for you. Records show that you were dismissed by Beryl

346

Cleveland. Being fired usually leaves rancour with an employee. Some months later you started for Mrs. Darricourt. At that time her husband — you, Mr. Morton — was in prison serving five years for embezzlement. I'll hazard a guess that you entered the Darricourt family to later get your own back on Beryl Cleveland, and that it was you who introduced her name to Mr. Morton here when he came out of prison. You knew him to be a stockbroker, naturally.'

'Yes,' Bella muttered. 'I did it with the fixed intention of having the master take the wind out of Miss Cleveland's sails. To fleece her, to be exact. I knew he could, and that he would not be too particular how he did it. He was quite willing.'

Morton sat eyeing the maid stonily, his lips tight.

'And then?' Garth questioned.

'Things went wrong. She stood to clean up a fortune and ruin the master, instead of the other way round. There was only one way to stop that — be rid of her. I'd no objections. I hated the sight of her. Then Mrs. Morton here — Hazel Jackson as she was then — came into the picture. She said — being fully determined to marry the master — that she wouldn't have him without money. She had the charm necessary to cultivate Miss Cleveland, and so finally get her to the right spot. She arranged a meeting for that night and we picked up Miss Cleveland on our way out of town, together with Mrs. Morton — Miss Jackson — who had brought her there.'

Garth nodded. 'Just as I'd thought. A triumvirate. Then she was strangled, but unfortunately for you Collins came across the body, got a statement out of her before she died, removed her in his car to your house, Mr. Morton, and ever since that time blackmailed you. You had to pay, because you couldn't find where the indictment was hidden.'

'This is still without proof,' Morton said grimly.

Garth felt inside his pocket and produced a piece of creased, rolled-up paper.

'I wouldn't have been so positive in my accusations if I hadn't have been sure.

This has been found, but I've no intention of gratifying your curiosity as to where. Listen to this — '

He flattened the note on the blotter and read:

'I, Beryl Cleveland, hereby swear that I was this night attacked with intent to murder by Vincent Darricourt, who tried to strangle me and then threw me out of his car into a ditch, and he was assisted in this by Bella Gibson, my former maid, and Hazel Jackson, whom I had always thought my close friend. Signed Beryl Cleveland and dated August ninth, nineteen . . . '

'Doesn't prove a thing,' Morton interrupted angrily. 'Anybody could write that.'

'This was written by Collins and signed by Beryl Cleveland,' Garth replied. 'Collins was smart enough to use a page of his diary for that year. It can be traced back to the manufacturers and the format for that year can be checked. The signature of Beryl Cleveland can be proved against the documents from her home, at her lawyer's, and at the bank.

Even the age of the ink can be given within a month or two . . . There's no doubt, Morton, you attempted the murder of Beryl Cleveland.'

'Which,' Morton said, 'isn't actual murder. Collins himself could have finished her off afterwards when he hanged her in my home.'

'I agree,' Garth conceded. 'We can never be sure. It's for a court to decide. That doesn't concern me. My interest now shifts to Granville Collins . . . ' He held the diary-indictment in the air. 'This note was the one thing you three here wanted from Collins and until you found it you had only two alternatives — pay what he demanded — since obviously you knew what was in the note, for he must have read it to you sometime — until you got hold of it; or else murder him and get it that way. True, the note does not indict you for murder only attempted murder, but even that is a grave charge and none of you wanted to face the consequences. And of course the woman had died subsequently . . .

'Unfortunately for you Collins was

350

wary — a man who suffered from claustrophobia, and for that reason rarely went anywhere beyond his home or office. At his office there were many other people in the building. At home he always slept with a gun. Yet you had to *get* him — and of late it became urgent. You, Morton, with your business going on the rocks had simultaneously received a demand from Collins for more money.'

Morton smiled coldly, said nothing

'I base that assumption on the fact that Collins had told his wife he was definitely going to improve conditions all round,' Garth continued. 'Briefly, he *had* to if he was to retain his hold on her: there was a growing rift between them. He raised the price — and you, needing every penny you could get to make a comeback knew that you couldn't pay it. There was only one way — murder him somewhere quiet where you could get that confession from his person before it could be found.

'You planned very carefully. One slip would land the lot of you at the mercy of Collins and his indictment would be handed over to the police. You found out which route he took to the office each day and selected the quietest spot on the route — Back Mercer Street. You did more: you found out just where to put a revolver so you wouldn't have to carry it before or after the crime. A thirty-eight won't fit easily in a pocket. Long ago that gun was bought under an alias . . .

'Next, you did your best to make sure the police would be diverted by sending a typewritten note, which you, Bella, typed.' Garth looked at her. 'You needn't deny it. You should have known that no typewriter, not even a new one, is unique.'

There was a gathering tension in the office. Garth hunched forward.

'Unfortunately for you, things went wrong. Collins was shot, yes, but he didn't die as you'd anticipated. Instead he died in his office.'

'Why?' Morton asked incautiously.

'You'll hear the explanation later — in court,' Garth retorted. 'The point is: you didn't get the indictment after all because your plan fell to bits through an occurrence you could never have foreseen. You thought Collins would die, or at least collapse, in Back Mercer Street where you could have a few, quiet un-overlooked moments to search him. I doubt if you would ever have found the indictment, but that is by the way now.'

Morton smiled bitterly. 'You have a singular disregard for facts Inspector! I can have the law on you for this. I have a perfectly sound alibi, and so has my wife . . . '

Garth ignored him and got to his feet. Then he said quietly, 'Hazel Morton, I arrest you for the murder of Granville Collins, and I have to warn you that anything you say will be taken down in writing and may be used as evidence at your trial.'

Sergeant Whittaker thought that in that moment he had never known the grubby old office to be so utterly quiet.

21

It was half an hour later before Garth and Whittaker were alone again in the office. Following the charge of murder against Hazel Morton, Dudley Morton and Bella Gibson had also been charged with complicity and duly removed. Now Garth sat in his swivel chair, crackling a cheroot between his fingers.

'You see, Whitty, even though I was more or less certain that Hazel Morton was guilty, she admitted the fact herself. Which was just what I wanted.'

'You mean when she confessed, sir?' Whittaker looked at his notebook.

'No, before that. When she said that to the best of her knowledge Collins always dressed in black coat and vest with striped trousers, bowler hat, and white handkerchief in his breast pocket. That was wrong, you see. As a rule he *never* wore a white handkerchief in his breast pocket; he hated the idea. He only wore it on the morning of his death because it was the outcome of a domestic tiff. Only one person outside of the police and Mrs. Collins knew that he was wearing it that morning — and that was the killer.'

'I get it now,' Whittaker said.

'The alibi they cooked up between them was fairly smart,' Garth went on, 'but against scientific equipment it doesn't stand five minutes. It was *Bella* who telephoned that morning, in lieu of Mrs. Morton. They were fully confident that Morton's staff would say it was Mrs. Morton. A telephone is not the best medium by which to judge a voice, anyway, and to imitate her gushing style wasn't difficult to a woman of resource, and one who'd known her for years. Let me show you something, Whitty. Come with me.'

Garth led the way down the corridor to the projection theatre where Pierce was waiting. He stirred from his seat as the two men came in. Garth nodded to him.

'All right, Pierce, let's have it. Sit down, Whitty,' he added.

Whittaker settled next to Garth. The

lights dimmed as Pierce spoke a few words into the telephone. As on the earlier occasion when Garth had made his own preview there appeared on the top half of the screen the 'peak and valley' view of sound track.

'That,' Pierce said, 'is Morton's voice in light reproduction, taken from the Dictaphone recording. And here' — he pressed a button beside the 'phone — 'is the same voice recorded in the Inspector's office yesterday morning when Morton called.'

A second length of valley and peak track appeared, and certain peaks and valleys matched identically.

'Scientifically, in any court of law, that is Morton's voice in both cases,' Garth's voice said out of the gloom. 'No two voices are alike no matter how you disguise them.'

'I understand, sir,' Whittaker said. 'Did you show this lot to Mrs. Morton and her husband?'

'Like hell! They'll find out all about it at the trial.'

'Here,' Pierce said, as the scene changed, 'is the voice of the woman who spoke on the telephone to Morton, and here underneath it, is the voice of Bella Gibson, as it was recorded in the Chief Inspector's office yesterday evening. They check in twenty fundamentals. Where they don't check is in the places where Bella Gibson tried to disguise it, but no human being can alter the utterance of certain syllables, or the length of the vocal chords that are responsible for the height or depth of a voice. Bella Gibson spoke over the 'phone to Morton, and incidentally to the Dictaphone.'

The lower checking image was withdrawn and another one slid into place.

'This,' Garth said, 'is Mrs. Morton's voice, when she arrived this morning, though I already knew she hadn't spoken to her husband over the phone on the morning of the murder. I told Dr. Pierce here to rush through a print copy of the first few words to make a check up. The rest of the conversation was recorded in the usual way. Here it is.'

'And not one item checks,' Pierce added quietly.

The screen blanked and the lights came

up. They left the projection theatre and when Garth was back again in his swivel chair he said,

'Fortunately, the thought of being left holding the bag stung Mrs. Morton into a confession. Just read over what she said, will you?'

'Yes, sir.' Whittaker picked up his notebook. ''It was his idea! The alibi, I mean! All right, so you charge me with Collins's murder. Yes, I *did* shoot him. I fully intended to! You don't think I'm going to be left holding the bag while my husband and maid get lesser sentences, do you? Not likely! Collins raised his demands by six times. It was impossible to pay him. We had to get rid of him. We planned it pretty well — even as you've admitted, Inspector. I shot him with the thirty-eight as he came through Back Mercer Street. But nothing happened! I know I fired the bullet, and it should have gone straight to his heart. I'm an expert shot. My father was a gunsmith and he showed me all the tricks . . . I sighted a shade below the white handkerchief in his breast pocket. That's why I remember the handkerchief so well. He simply put a hand to his breast for a moment and I dodged back behind the parapet. He couldn't have seen me. He looked about him — and then to my amazement walked straight on! I didn't murder him! He wasn't even hurt!' Statement ends there, sir.'

Garth smiled coldly. 'I know why he walked on, Whitty, and so will the rest of 'em in court. Later I may be charging Morton with the murder of Beryl Cleveland as well. That has yet to be worked out with conclusive evidence.'

'Look, sir,' Whittaker said, 'I've got a few points down here which I can't answer myself. I'd hoped you'd help me.'

Garth grinned and lighted a cheroot appreciatively. 'Fire away!'

'First, I don't quite see how you tumbled to it that it was Mrs. Morton who did it.'

'Well, for no reason at all she was most anxious that I should see the document she had supposedly read to her husband, and for another she considered it an 'awfully lucky chance' that she had an alibi. Why should she say that? Because she was inwardly gloating over the fact that there was an apparently foolproof alibi. I suspected the alibi for the very reason that it was so good . . .

'Further, if the letter were as important as it was cracked up to be it would have come by registered post, and it didn't. Remember the 're-direction' stunt and the supposed stranger who brought it? They just saved themselves making a *faux pas* there. Again, had it been so important Morton, I don't think, would have entrusted it to a switchgirl and a Dictaphone. It was all for one reason only — to make an alibi. The maid, who had no alibi, was oddly enough suspected far less, as far as I was concerned.

'Again, only Mrs. Morton filled the bill because Morton had obviously not left his office. And it couldn't have been the maid because Howard Farrow referred to a 'small, slender figure' — and Bella Gibson is certainly not that!'

'Thank you, sir,' Whittaker said. 'And

you guessed her being a gunsmith's daughter was the answer to her being a crack shot.'

'Certainly. She said herself she had worked for her father until she was fifteen.'

'I see. Regarding the alibi — you decided to make a scientific check-up to be sure. And from that moment you had to work out what motive Mrs. Morton had?'

'Just that. I pieced together everything she said and traced it back — chiefly through noticing the formation of her husband's ear — to the 'Clothes Cupboard' mystery. In time Bella fitted into the picture, too.'

'Suppose that Beryl Cleveland would not have died had not Collins hanged her in the clothes cupboard? He himself might have been the murderer.'

'Hardly. She had, according to the medical report, been dead for nine hours. That, approximately, was the time she was strangled out in the country. For obvious reasons Collins could not bring her back to the Darricourt house until nightfall, which in August is not until about eleven to be really dark. That would make a difference of several hours in the time of death. No, Collins didn't murder her. He hung up a corpse.'

'Then what made you so sure *Collins* did that?'

'The clothes cupboard. To a man of his turn of mind, trying to prove murder, he wanted it to appear in its most diabolical form. To him, an enclosed cupboard was the most diabolical form, as well as being a good place of concealment where it would be some time before the body would be found, giving him ample time to get clear. What personal anguish he underwent working in that cupboard we shall never know. He certainly must have endured tortures, but the end justified the means.'

Whittaker brooded again. Then: 'How *did* Collins die, sir?'

Garth chuckled behind his cheroot. 'He was shot in Back Mercer Street, just as Mrs. Morton admitted, and the bullet entered the body just under the pulmonary vein area. There was very little blood. Now, Collins was a dyspeptic sufferer, even as I am. Occasionally that damned complaint gives you the hell of a momentary pain across the left top side of the breast. That, I believe — and Doc Myers bears me out on it — is what Collins felt. He must have heard the gun, of course — but he didn't see anything. And why should he suspect a *gun?* Might have been a backfire somewhere. Perhaps his chest was numbed, perhaps the pain was still there, but there wasn't enough blood to soak through to his outer coat that quickly. He went on his way and entered his office.

'All this time, though, the bullet was lodged a *fraction of an inch* above his heart. The smallest fraction, according to Dr. Myers' X-ray plates. Collins opened his matchboxes and went to the window, struggled and shoved to get it up. Then what? The strain he put on himself jerked the bullet down slightly in the tissue in which it rested and it lodged at the top of the heart, stopping its action. He fell dead, still holding the window sash. It slammed down with terrific force and there he lay — as we found him.'

'Hell!' Whittaker murmured. 'But that just couldn't happen!'

'It could, and it has, though not necessarily in regard to the heart.' Garth turned to the attache case he had brought and dragged out some books and newspaper cuttings. 'Listen here — This is what gave me the clue, and, checking with Dr. Myers later, I found it to be possible. First in this book of *Strange Accidents* by Fowler we have the following item — 'In the New York law court Douglas Grant was accused of the murder of Jonathan Strande by shooting him in the head, the bullet lodging in his brain. Later he was acquitted. The investigation showed the bullet was one from the First World War, and that for fifteen years Jonathan Strande had walked about with it in his skull. He slipped off a kerb and the jolt dislodged the bullet into his brain and killed him. Circumstantial evidence pinned the blame on Grant until these new facts came forth . . . '

'I can see that,' Whittaker admitted. 'Plenty of people today walking about with shrapnel in their bodies which might at any second move to a critical area and bring death or serious injury.'

'Exactly,' Garth agreed. 'Then there is this — in Ripley's *Believe It Or Not Omnibus:* 'Shineas Gage was charging a hole with powder preparatory to blasting. A premature explosion blew a tamping-iron, three feet seven long by one and a quarter inches thick through his head. He didn't even lose consciousness. All he did lose was one eye. The iron went right through his face and head, yet missed killing him and he went on all right afterwards'.'

Garth rustled the news cuttings.

'In this same field of the unusual we have the case of Beatrice Smith who in October nineteen thirty-five had apparently been strangled. Captain Peon proved that she hadn't — that asphyxia was due to an air embolism, a million to one chance. That's in the *Daily Express* for October twelfth of that year. Or later still — again in the *Express* for June fourth, nineteen forty-six, recall the case of Mason Berney of New York who shot himself through the mouth and was believed dead. He wasn't. The bullet went clean between the two lobes of his brain and had not affected either of them!'

Garth put the books and press cuttings back in the attaché case.

'These, Whitty, are only instances in the great pile of criminological data which proves the 'impossible' does happen now and again. In our particular case I reasoned from the premise that a bullet in the heart does not necessarily mean death, and sometimes not even unconsciousness. Nor is there much blood from a heart wound. Missing the pulmonary veins prevented that. Between Collins dying in Back Mercer Street and dying in his office there lay a thin layer of body tissue, which his struggle to open the window broke down — and then he died. Dr. Myers confirms this, and the erratic course of the bullet in Collins's body more or less shows how it entered with fair velocity, slowed down, and then jerked down the slight distance to the top of the heart. He'll testify to that in court.' Garth glanced at his watch. 'Anything else? I want my lunch . . . '

'No, sir. I must have been nuts not to have thought of it.'

Garth's eyes were gleaming as he got to his feet. 'Nuts? Whitty my boy, you've saved my life. That's the word I wanted for my crossword puzzle — !'

He headed for the door and Whittaker was left gazing blankly at a fragrant blue haze where his superior had been standing.

THE END

We do hope that you have enjoyed reading this large print book.

Did you know that all of our titles are available for purchase?

We publish a wide range of high quality large print books including:
Romances, Mysteries, Classics
General Fiction
Non Fiction and Westerns

Special interest titles available in large print are:
The Little Oxford Dictionary
Music Book, Song Book
Hymn Book, Service Book

Also available from us courtesy of Oxford University Press:
Young Readers' Dictionary
(large print edition)
Young Readers' Thesaurus
(large print edition)

For further information or a free brochure, please contact us at:
Ulverscroft Large Print Books Ltd.,
The Green, Bradgate Road, Anstey,
Leicester, LE7 7FU, England.
Tel: (00 44) **0116 236 4325**
Fax: (00 44) **0116 234 0205**

SCORPION: SECOND GENERATION

Michael R. Linaker

The colony of deadly scorpions at Long Point Nuclear Plant was eradicated. Or so people thought . . . Over a year later, entomologist Miles Ranleigh receives a worrying telephone call. A man has been fatally poisoned by toxic venom, identical to the Long Point scorpions' — but far more powerful. Miles and his companion Jill Ansty must race to destroy the fresh infestation. But this is a new strain of scorpion. Mutated and irradiated, they're larger, more savage — and infected with a deadly virus fatal to humans. And they're breeding . . .